THE CUCKOO SISTER

Vivien Alcock

THE CUCKOO SISTER

A Yearling Book

Published by
Dell Publishing
a division of
The Bantam Doubleday Dell Publishing Group, Inc.
666 Fifth Avenue
New York, New York 10103

This work was first published in Great Britain by Methuen
Children's Books Ltd.

ISBN: 0-440-40101-1

Reprinted by arrangement with Delacorte Press

Printed in the United States of America

November 1988

10 9 8 7 6 5 4 3 2 1

CW

The cuckoo lays her egg in another bird's nest
and flies away. And when the egg hatches,
the young cuckoo grows bigger and bigger, until one day
it pushes the true fledgling right out of the nest.

THE CUCKOO SISTER

1

The first of August had always been a bad day for us. I don't suppose I realized this when I was a baby. Babies are too dim and milky to know anything about calendars and dates. Yet perhaps even then I sensed something wrong; a tension in the hands that held me, wet, salty drops falling on my face from above.

However, I was five years old before I first noticed my mother cry. (How long ago that seems, now that I am fifteen.) I must have been pretty blind before then, because she cries a lot. It's her nerves. Any little thing will set her off. Her life is full of last straws; a run in her stocking, a broken fingernail, me. . . . To be honest, it's mostly me.

I've been pretty horrid to her since I found out what had happened. It might have been different if they had told me themselves and not let me hear about it by accident. It *was* by accident. I wasn't eavesdropping, not then. I was a friendly, innocent child in those days.

I had been playing in the garden. It was a hot day, I remember. My hands were as slippery as butter. The yellow ball slid through them and rolled across the grass into the flowerbed beneath the window. I followed it. The lavender bushes were gigantic then, their huge smoky spires high above my head and the air thick with their heavy scent. I have always hated the smell of lavender since that day.

The window above me was open. As I knelt on the

hard-baked earth, searching for my ball, I heard my
father's voice. I hardly recognized it. It sounded different. Not angry exactly, but odd, tight, like a wire about
to snap.

"Yes, I do know it's the first of August. I'm hardly
likely to forget it, am I?" he was saying. "For God's sake,
Margaret, must you start crying again? . . . It's been
seven years, after all. Isn't it time we began to . . ."

"To forget? Is that what you were going to say?"
My mother's voice sounded terrible, shrill and wobbly.
It frightened me. "You want me to forget my own
child? As if she was a lost umbrella?"

They were talking about me. They must be—I was
their only child. They thought I was lost, but I wasn't. I
was just hidden by the lavender. I had only to call out
and say "I'm here, Mummy" and everything would be
all right.

But I didn't. I crouched there, horribly frightened,
listening to their unfamiliar voices. I no longer tried to
see over the windowsill. I think I was afraid they would
be changed into some sort of monsters, like in fairy tales
where nothing is what it seems to be. Why did my
father want Mummy to forget me? What had I done? I
couldn't remember anything particularly bad, but I was
too young to be sure. People often said, "No, don't do
that, dear. That's naughty," and it was news to me. I
had no certainty of the difference between right and
wrong.

I don't remember now exactly what they said. A lot
of it didn't seem to make sense. But then I heard my
father say, "It would be easier, wouldn't it, if we knew
that she was dead. It's not knowing that's so terrible."

It was the worst moment in my life. I was so terrified that I wet myself. And that was bad. I knew that
was bad. It was no good running crying to Mummy for

comfort. She wouldn't love me now. Daddy didn't love me. He hated me. He wanted me dead. Nobody loved me. I stood there, trembling and crying, a right little misery, wet at both ends. I can laugh now, looking back at myself, but remember, I was only five. That was the first time I ran away.

I didn't get far. Only to the corner of the road. There were two crossings, one in each direction. I knew traffic was supposed to stop for people there. It didn't stop for me. As I stood there, wondering what to do, a loud voice said, "It's Kate, isn't it? Yes, it is. What are you doing out by yourself?"

I looked up, startled. It was Miss Wait. She is my godmother, a sort of relation of Daddy's, who lives in the country and comes to see us when she's in town. I had been told to call her Aunt Elizabeth, but I never would. I didn't like her then, you see. She is a large square woman with a weatherbeaten face, on which a sprinkling of powder lies like dust on mahogany. She drinks a lot of whiskey and talks about dogs and horses. I didn't think she had ever noticed me. She had never talked to me before, not even to say hello when she saw me. I could have been a chair or a small table—I used to think if I stood still long enough she might put her glass down on my head by mistake.

I didn't answer. I didn't know what to say. I just stood there crying. My nose was running and I put out my tongue to lick away the snot.

"Disgusting child," Miss Wait said, not sounding too upset about it. "Haven't you a hanky? Silly question. Of course you haven't. Kids never have. Here, take mine." And she handed me a large white handkerchief as big as a tablecloth.

I blew my nose and mopped up my face a bit, and offered it back.

"Ugh, no, thank you. Get your mother to wash it first," she said.

I started sniveling again. "Mummy doesn't love me," I mumbled, meaning that because of this she was not likely to wash anything for me anymore, and so if Miss Wait wanted her hanky back, she'd better take it now or it would be lost and dirty for ever. I don't know if she followed this reasoning. She just said, "Don't be silly. Of course she does."

She sounded so sure. She always did. She was the sort of woman who believed in telling people things to their faces, and was often rude. "What on earth made you buy that dress?" she'd said to my mother once. "You look a positive fright in it." I'd thought she was beastly. But now she seemed like a rock in a dissolving world.

"Come and have an ice cream," she said. "Ice cream is the cure for all the ills of childhood." I really believed her, as if she were a doctor and ice cream a new medicine. I went with her. I didn't have much choice. My hand was firmly held in her huge red one. It was oddly comforting, that large, red hand. I didn't want to escape. I think I was already frightened of running away.

She took me to an ice cream parlor and lifted me onto one of those very high stools with a single metal leg attached to the floor. She did not ask me what I wanted but chose for me, an enormous ice cream in a tall glass, with streaks of chocolate and raspberry sauce and cherries on the top. She herself only had coffee. I suppose they did not sell whiskey. She sat sipping it, and balancing the wrapped lumps of sugar one on top of the other. She didn't say anything until I was halfway through my ice cream. Then she said, "You've got chocolate on your dress. Mop it up, there's a good girl."

I scrubbed at it with her handkerchief, looking up at her through my lashes, thinking, I suppose she'll start on at me now. The ice cream had given me courage. I thought about running away again. But the floor looked a long way down, and the door to the street seemed a mile away.

"What was all that sniveling about?" she asked. She didn't sound very interested. Perhaps that's what made me tell her. Nobody likes to be thought a bore.

"Daddy wants me dead," I said.

I watched her face. I expected her to be shocked, horrified. I was reassured when she smiled. Not nastily. More as if we were friends and she had something nice to tell me.

"Nonsense," she said. "You've got hold of the wrong end of the stick. Children always do. Did myself at your age."

"I heard him! I heard him say so!"

"Shouldn't listen behind doors. Can't hear properly through keyholes. Hear a bit of this and a bit of that and add it together all wrong. I know. I heard my father say once, when I was your age, 'She's an ugly brute. I don't think I'll keep her.' Cried for a week—thought he was talking about me, you see. Always knew I was ugly. It turned out he was talking about a new chestnut mare he'd bought. Funny, even when I found this out, I never quite forgave him. Children are queer cattle."

I stared at her. I'd often thought she was an ugly old bag. I'd never wondered before whether she minded. I felt so sorry for her that new tears came into my eyes, pushing out the ones that had been for myself.

"Stop drizzling. You're worse than a wet Sunday,"

she said. "Bet they weren't even talking about you at all. Fifty to one. Can't say fairer than that, can I?"

"They were talking about me. We haven't even got a horse. It was me."

"You're not the only Kate in the world, you know. Plenty of Kates about. Know five of 'em myself. Five and a half, if I count you."

"It was me," I said angrily. "Mummy didn't say anything about Kate. She said—she said Daddy wanted her to forget her own child. And that's me." I began to cry again.

She stared at me. For the first time I felt I had all her attention, and it was overwhelming. Then she said, "What's the date? It's August first, isn't it? You poor little devil, they weren't talking about you, they were talking about Emma. It's her birthday today. The first of August."

"Emma?"

"You know. Emma. Your sister," she added as I gaped at her. "Don't tell me they've never told you about her?"

"I haven't got a sister," I said. "I'm an only child."

"Good Lord. Put my foot in it, haven't I? Still, you were bound to find out sooner or later. Can't think why they didn't tell you themselves. Better to know about things. Stops you worrying. Or at least lets you know what to worry about." She stopped and gazed at me, chewing her lip as if it were a stick of gum. Then she said, "Might as well tell you now. Your parents had another child before you were born. A baby girl. Emma. But, well, your mother lost her . . ."

"She's dead?"

"No. If she'd died, I'd have said so. I'm not frightened of using the proper words for things. Lost. Your mother left her in her pram outside a dress shop. She

wanted some new dresses now she'd lost her bulge—
you do know where babies come from, I hope?" I nodded, and reassured, she went on, "When your mother
came out of the shop, there was just the empty pram.
No baby."

My tears had dried up. I was fascinated and bewildered, perched on my high stool, with my mouth open
and the taste of chocolate still on my lips.

"Where had the baby gone?" I asked. "My sister," I
added, trying the words and liking them. They tasted of
the chocolate. I saw her as a small baby. I didn't realize
she would have grown.

"I don't know. She was never found. It wasn't a
kidnaping, as far as anyone could tell. There was no
ransom demand . . ."

"What?"

"Ransom—don't you ever watch telly? Oh, well,
never mind. The police thought it was probably some
poor madwoman who'd lost her own baby."

"But she shouldn't take Mummy's. That's stealing,"
I said, shocked.

"Yes."

"Can't we get her back?"

"Kate, this happened years ago, before you were
born. Everything possible was done then, the police,
private detectives, everything, but there was no trace
of her. She's almost certainly . . . O Lord, I wish I
hadn't started this."

"I want my sister," I said. "I want her."

I think I thought of her as a sort of cuddly toy I
could carry about. I did not realize she would be older
than me.

"That's enough of that," Miss Wait said firmly.
"You're putting it on. I can tell. If you don't shut up this

minute, I'll cut you up in small pieces and feed you to my dogs."

Though she smiled as she said this, I half believed she would. Not wanting to risk it, I was silent, chewing the end of her handkerchief.

"I wish I hadn't told you," Miss Wait said. "I thought you were old enough to be sensible about it." She looked at me hopefully. I don't think I could have looked very sensible, because she sighed and said, "I'm in for trouble. Your father will be furious with me."

"Did he hate her?" I asked.

"Of course not. Don't be silly. He adored her."

"Why does he want to forget her, then?"

She took my sticky hands in hers and said very seriously, "Kate, it was a terrible thing to happen, but it's over now. Past. Finished. Your parents have suffered enough. The best thing we can all do is to try to forget it."

I did not say anything. I think I must have looked stubborn. I thought, I'm never going to forget my sister. Never. Poor little Emma, I promise I won't forget you.

It was one of the few promises I kept.

2

One day in July, when I was eleven years old, Miss Wait came up to London especially to see me. My father was out at work. My mother had gone to one of her painting classes. When I told Miss Wait this, hoping she would go away, she said, "Good. It's you I've come to see, Kate. I want to talk to you. Let's go into the garden."

I followed her reluctantly. I expected she wanted

to give me a talking to. People were always trying to do that. It was boring.

She sat in a garden chair in the shade, and I lay on the dry yellow grass beside her. It was very hot. The leaves above our heads hung limp and motionless beneath a heavy sky. I thought I could smell lavender. I shut my eyes, prepared to let her reproaches wash over me. I'd heard it all before. I knew it by heart.

Somehow, since the day I found out about Emma, I seemed to have gone to the bad. I was rude. I told lies. I listened at doors and read other people's letters if they left them about. Not that they did anymore. Not since the time I read a letter from Aunt Mary suggesting I should be sent to boarding school to be knocked into shape. After the fuss I made, my father was careful to lock his letters in his desk.

I was always losing things, presents people had gone to great trouble and expense to get me: watches, cameras, and silver bracelets. And whenever my mother reproached me, I screamed at her, "Look who's talking! Who lost her own baby? Who lost my sister? Just because you wanted a new dress."

My mother would go off somewhere to cry, and my father would shut his mouth tightly, so that I knew he was swearing inside himself. Then he'd take me into his study and talk to me very seriously and sadly for a long time, while I tried not to listen.

I used to hate the sound of his voice when he was being patient. He spoke through his teeth. I think he was afraid to open his mouth wider in case something horrible slipped out. I knew he was disappointed in me. He didn't have to tell me so. I bet he wished it was me who got lost instead of Emma.

"Can't you see what it's doing to your mother,

Kate?" he said. "You don't want her to be ill again, do you?"

No, I thought, I love her. I don't mean to hurt her.

But I never said this aloud. I don't know why. It's always the wrong words that slide so easily off my tongue. The right ones, the ones I know would earn my gold stars of approval, seem to stick in my throat.

"Please try harder, Kate," my father used to say. "We must help one another put this unhappy business behind us. We're a family."

I think that was the trouble. We were not a family. We were incomplete. When we sat at the table, we only took up three sides of it. There was an empty space where Emma would have sat. There was an unused bedroom next to mine where Emma would have slept. Every Christmas I got twice as many presents as any of my friends, and when I arranged them in my room, I thought, half of these are Emma's. That's her doll. That's her book. Those painting things were really meant for her. . . .

In the streets, in the parks, there were too many children who might have been Emma. Girls who looked a little like me. I have straight fair hair and gray-blue eyes. There are hundreds like me. And sometimes one of them would stare back, as if she recognized me. When I was younger, I could not help tugging my mother's sleeve and crying out, "Mummy, it's Emma!"

I didn't do that anymore now. My life was more interesting, what with my friends and school. I went to Queen Charlotte's, a private day school for girls. Our uniform was brown, the blazer piped with pale blue and a fancy crest on the pocket. "A school for young ladies," Mrs. Trapp, our cleaning woman, called it, with a slight edge to her voice that my mother never seemed to notice.

Mrs. Trapp was always telling me how lucky I was, with my lovely home, holidays abroad twice a year, and all my toys. Once, when I'd been whining about something, she told me sharply that her niece's children would give their eyeteeth for half of what I had. So I packed a large box with toys I'd hardly ever played with and asked her to give it to them. But that was wrong too.

She went bright red and said that she hadn't been hinting. Her niece was perfectly able to give her children all they needed, thank you. If I wanted to give my old toys away, there was always Oxfam. Or some other charity. I hadn't meant to offend her, so I cried and she forgave me.

"You mustn't think I grudge you anything, dear," she said. "After all, money isn't everything, is it?"

"No," I agreed eagerly. "I'd much rather have my little sister than all my toys."

I'd overdone it again. She pushed me away, saying tartly, "You've played that tune too often, my girl."

She seemed to think that, having so much, I had no right to complain. About anything. Ever. Yet somehow I never felt myself to be lucky. I don't know why. I was happy enough most of the time, I suppose.

Often weeks would go by and I never thought of Emma at all. But I still dreamed about her. Silly dreams. Sometimes she would come back in a Rolls-Royce, driven by a chauffeur. The car would be loaded with presents. Sometimes the woman who had stolen her had become a famous film star and they wanted me to go and live with them in Hollywood.

But sometimes Emma came back as a baby, dirty, neglected, thin as a ghost. She came tapping at our door with fingers like peeled sticks, mewing like a cat. And my father would say, "Don't listen. Don't let her in. We must put her behind us."

A shoe nudged my leg, and Miss Wait said, "Have you gone to sleep? I was talking to you, Kate."

I opened my eyes. The sun had drained all color out of the world. My arm was silver. Miss Wait in her chair looked like a great gray hippopotamus.

"I was thinking about my sins," I said. "Isn't that what you wanted me to do?"

"Sisters," she said. "All this fuss about sisters. I've got three of 'em. Have one. Have 'em all. Can't stand the sight of them myself."

I didn't want one of her sisters. I wanted one of my own.

"You don't understand," I said. It was my favorite defense. It put grown-ups in their place; clumsy, prehistoric creatures too thick to understand an intricate and mysterious person like me. It was guaranteed to annoy them.

"I understand all right," Miss Wait said. "You're just using Emma as a stick to beat your parents with. I know. Kids always hit below the belt if you give 'em half a chance. Can't reach any higher, I suppose."

I did not mind her rudeness. I found the fact that she expected children to be dirty, noisy, and badly behaved rather restful. I did not have to live up to expectations. I could roll in the mud, if I wanted to, like one of her puppies.

"It's not like that," I said.

"What is it like?"

"I can't explain."

"Try."

I did not want to. It was so hot. My brain was melting like ice cream in the sun. "Oh, it's just . . . we're not a proper family. I mean, not like my friends have."

"In what way?"

"I don't know. . . . There's something missing. A sort of empty space. It's there all the time, and we're not supposed to talk about it. We never talk properly, never. We're too polite—except when I lose my temper, and then I make Mummy cry. I don't mean to—her name sort of slips out. Emma's, I mean. She's always there waiting. . . . Sometimes when I go upstairs to bed, I think—" I broke off, afraid to go on in case she laughed at me.

Instead she quoted,

"As I was going up the stair,
I met a man who wasn't there.
He wasn't there again today.
I wish that man would go away."

"Yes," I said eagerly. "It's exactly like that."

"That's just a nursery rhyme. Babies' stuff," Miss Wait said briskly. "What are you now? Ten? Eleven?"

"Eleven."

"Too old for that sort of nonsense. It's unhealthy. Gets on people's nerves. I feel responsible. Your father has never forgiven me for telling you. But how was I to know you were going to make such a goose of yourself? All this 'my poor little lost sister' stuff. Nauseating. Enough to turn anyone's stomach. No wonder your mother looks like a dishrag. You've got to promise to stop it."

I shut my eyes and did not answer. She prodded me with her toe.

"Kate, come on. I'm not leaving here until you've promised."

"How can I promise to forget her? You can't forget to order."

"I'm not asking you to forget. You can think about her all you like. Dream about her, fill your silly head with romantic notions. I don't care. But stop talking about her. Stop dragging her name into every row you have with your mother. You can keep your mouth shut, I hope? Haven't got adenoids, have you?"

"No," I said. I couldn't help smiling.

"Will you promise?" she asked, and when I hesitated, added gently, "Kate, the police think Emma is dead. They think she must have died soon after she was taken. They would have found her otherwise. Or the woman who took her would have come to her senses and given her back. That's what usually happens, apparently. I'm sorry, but it's better to face facts. Emma is dead. It is no good expecting her back."

Perhaps, at that very moment, the woman was writing her letter on the bright-blue lined writing paper. I wonder what the girl was doing? Leaning over her shoulder, reading what the woman was writing, and laughing? No, I don't think she could have been laughing. She never laughs. . . .

You see, a week after Miss Wait said this, Emma turned up. At least, someone has turned up. I'm not certain who she is. I don't believe she's really Emma at all.

3

The envelope was the first thing we saw. My mother and I were having lunch under the elderberry tree. It had not rained for weeks and the garden was looking depressed. The lettuce on my plate was limp, the ham sweating. A small spider walked quickly over my hard-boiled egg.

"Aren't you hungry, darling?" my mother asked.

"It's so hot."

"Try to eat a little."

"All right."

We were both being careful. It was the first of August, Emma's birthday, the dangerous day. We were determined not to quarrel.

I could hear Mrs. Trapp banging saucepans about in the kitchen. She never has lunch with us, though my mother always asks her to.

"I'll have a little something when I get home," she says. She is a liar. She goes to the pub on Heath Street. I saw her there through the door once. She was eating fish and chips and laughing loudly with someone I couldn't see. There was a glass of some dark liquid, like Coke only with foam on top, on the table beside her. I envied her. When I'm grown up, I'll go to the pub with my friends and roar with laughter, slapping my knee with my hand. I won't stay at home, sipping water out of a crystal glass and making stilted conversation.

My mother was fiddling with her hair, twisting a strand around her finger. Her hands are always restless, picking at a loose thread, tearing a leaf, or rolling the bread into small gray pellets. Playing for sympathy. It gets on my nerves sometimes.

"It's so humid, isn't it?" she said.

"Yes."

"They said there'd be thunder tonight. I hope so. It will clear the air."

"It could do with it."

Mrs. Trapp came through the French window and

started walking across the lawn towards us. I thought she had finished and was coming for her money. Then I noticed the envelope in her hands. In the dull, dusty summer garden, it looked brilliantly blue. I don't think I had a premonition. It was the bright color that attracted me.

"A child brought this to the door," Mrs. Trapp said, holding it out to my mother. "Says she's to wait for an answer."

"A child?" My mother looked round vaguely, as if she thought the child might be hiding behind a bush.

"I told her to wait outside. And I shut the front door," Mrs. Trapp said darkly. She was always afraid we were going to be robbed. She did not trust anyone.

"It might be one of my friends," I said.

"No." Mrs. Trapp shook her head decidedly. "I don't think so, dear."

My mother had opened the letter. The blue paper was fluttering and jumping in her shaking hand. Even her face seemed to reflect the cold color. She looked queer.

"What's the matter, Mummy?" I asked.

She got to her feet and looked wildly round. "Where's Anthony? Oh, why isn't he here?"

Anthony is my father's name. "Daddy's at the office," I pointed out, a little frightened. "What is it? What's the matter?"

Her lips trembled. "Emma," she said, and fainted.

She did not fall right down. She swayed forwards, bumping against the table and setting everything rattling. Mrs. Trapp caught her and lowered her onto her chair. "Put your head down between your knees, dear," she said, her arm round my mother's shoulders. "That helps. Makes the blood come to your head."

It wasn't the first time my mother had fainted. I knew Mrs. Trapp could look after her. The letter was lying on the grass at my feet. I picked it up and held it out of sight.

"I'll get some brandy," I said, and ran into the house.

I went into the dining room and looked out of the window. My mother was leaning forward, her head in her hands, and Mrs. Trapp was patting her shoulder. I poured a little brandy into a glass and left it on the sideboard. Then I read the letter.

It was not easy to make out. Though the writing was large and round, the ink did not show up clearly against the blue paper, and it was smudged as if it had been left out in the rain. Also it went on and on; for the first time I saw the sense in having punctuation.

Dear mrs seton
    you wont never forgive me i know i done a wicked thing it was me wot took yor baby i went funny when baby died wich was why i done it i was afrayed they put me in prison if i sed wot i done and i dint want to give her back i loved her like mine but i feel bad about it its not fair on rosie being so poor my man friend left me and i got no money and i red in the paper sunday how you never got over it so i am sending her back to you better late than never

yours faithful
Louise

p s please love her she is a good girl tell her to forget me i am going away so its no good her come looking for me i wont be there

I had to read it twice. I was so excited I could not make any sense of it at first. Even the second time I wasn't sure whose baby had died or who Rosie was.

I turned the letter over and saw there was more writing on the back:

> i dint know wot you call her i call her rosie it was my poor babys name but the paper sed emma

"Emma!" I cried.

I dropped the letter, rushed into the hall, and flung open the front door. Then I stopped and stood there, staring. My mind was blank except for one word, NO.

The girl was standing with her back to me, scraping the gravel into patterns with her foot. She was terribly thin, with short, spiky dark hair. Though her clothes were clean, they didn't seem to fit her. Her frilly nylon blouse was too big, her pink skirt too skimpy. She had clean white ankle socks and scuffed off-white shoes. The high heels were so badly worn down that her bony ankles were bent over sideways. Her legs and arms were like sticks, the skin sallow and rather dirty-looking.

When she turned round, I saw she was wearing makeup, blue eye shadow and a lipstick so pale it looked as if she had been drinking bleach. Beneath her ragged fringe, her eyes were dark gray and hard as pebbles. She did not smile at me but said sharply, " 'Oo d'you think you're staring at?" It was a good question.

"You're not Emma," I cried. "You're *not!*"

"Never said I was, did I? I'm Rosie, if it's any of your business. Mum said I got to wait for an answer. You got it? I can't hang about all day, you know."

I could not speak. I was terribly disappointed.

My mother and Mrs. Trapp came up behind me. I

turned. My mother was looking at the girl. I saw the
expression fresh on her face. I'm not stupid. I'm very
clever at guessing what people are thinking even when
they pretend otherwise. I'm certain that her first
thought was the same as mine. NO.

Mrs. Trapp muttered in my ear, "Your dad's coming right away. We rang him up."

I did not look at her. I was watching my mother's
face. Now she was looking confused, like an actress who
had thought she knew her lines but found herself in the
wrong play. I wondered if she had imagined the scene
as often as I had, if she too had dreamed of Emma
coming back. My mother is very soft. I expect her
dreams were all hugging and kissing, laughing and crying. My baby. My lost baby.

But this was no baby on the gravel drive. It was a
thin, spiky stranger with hard eyes.

"It isn't Emma, Mummy," I said, meaning to comfort her. "She's too old." I thought the girl was fifteen or
sixteen at least.

My mother took no notice of me. She drew a short
breath, as if she were screwing up her courage. Like
when you're on the high diving board and there are
people coming up behind you, and you know it's now or
never. Then, before I could stop her, she ran down the
steps, saying in a high, stagey voice, "My dear, I'm so
glad . . ." and tried to put her arms round the girl. Just
in case she was Emma.

The girl jumped back, quick as an animal, and my
mother was left with her arms in the air. I wanted to
giggle. I'm not heartless, but it was funny, honestly.
None of us knowing quite what to do, and the girl staring at us as if we were all mad.

"Mum told me to wait for an answer," she said,

keeping a wary eye on my mother as if afraid she might spring at her again.

There was a pause. Then my mother said, sounding amazed, as if she could hardly believe it, "But—don't you know what's in the letter?"

"No. I don't read other people's letters, do I? If there ain't an answer, missus, I'll be off."

I couldn't see my mother's face now, her back was towards me, but I heard her voice when she said, "Oh, no! my poor child. How could she do it like this? How could she?" She sounded as if she were going to cry.

"I'm off," the girl said, backing away, and muttered under her breath, "Bleeding nutters."

It was Mrs. Trapp who came to our rescue.

"You come back here, my girl," she said firmly. "If your mum said you was to wait for an answer, you wait for one. Have you had lunch?"

The girl hesitated. If she'd decided to run, we would not have had a chance to catch her. But she seemed reassured by Mrs. Trapp. Or perhaps she was being sly? Perhaps it was all an act?

"Yeh. Well, I had a packet of crisps," she said.

"That's not enough to put flesh on your bones, is it? Come into the kitchen with me and I'll give you a sandwich and a glass of milk while you wait. Mr. Seton won't be long."

"There's some cold chicken," I offered. I wanted her to stay. I had got over my first disappointment that it wasn't Emma, and was excited. I could hardly wait for my father to come back. He's not soft like my mother. I don't mean he's unkind, but he's a lawyer. He would know what to do. I longed to see his face when he found out what had happened.

"Please come in," my mother said softly. "Rosie— it's Rosie, isn't it?"

"Yeh," the girl said. "Well, all right. I don't mind if I do."

We encouraged her. We did it ourselves. We invited the cuckoo into our nest.

4

"I don't believe it. *She*'s not your sister," Mrs. Trapp said. She must have read the letter too. She seemed to know all about it. Unless my mother had told her. "If you ask me, they're just up to no good."

We were alone in the kitchen. Mrs. Trapp had sent the girl, whoever she was, to wash her hands. Then she had settled my mother on the sofa in the living room, telling her so decidedly that she looked ill that my mother turned quite pale and leaned back against the cushions obediently. I think she was glad of an excuse to do nothing until my father came.

"I know she's not Emma. She's too old for one thing," I said.

To my surprise, Mrs. Trapp did not agree immediately.

"How old would Emma be now?" she asked.

"Thirteen. Thirteen today. It's her birthday."

"Oh, well, she's about the right age, then," Mrs. Trapp said grudgingly. "No more than twelve or thirteen, I shouldn't think. Once you've washed the muck off her face. They often look older, you know."

"They? Who?"

"Slum kids," she said briefly, then added, "Poor little devils."

I did not want her to sympathize with the girl.

"But what are they doing it for?" I asked.

"I expect they read all about it in the Sundays and thought they were on to a good thing."

"What good thing?" I asked, puzzled.

Mrs. Trapp shrugged. "Thievery, I shouldn't be surprised. Your mum and dad didn't ought to let her stay in the house tonight, or she'll be sneaking down the stairs when you're asleep and letting them in."

"Oh," I said. I was half frightened, half excited. "But how did they know about us? It's years and years since there was anything in the papers. Before I was born," I added regretfully.

Mrs. Trapp shook her head. "Last Sunday. I saw it myself. Mrs. Seton won't like that, I thought, bringing it all up again. There was another baby gone from her pram last week, you see. Though they got that one back. And there was this article all about similar cases. Your mum was in it. Said as how she'd never got over it. Don't know how they knew. I never told no one. Still, it was an easy guess."

"I never saw it."

"Different paper, I expect. Don't worry, dear. Your dad will sort it out when he comes. Famous lawyer, they called him. He won't let them put anything over, I'm sure."

"I wonder if . . ." I began, but Mrs. Trapp said, "Sh-hh!" and put her finger to her lips.

A door had shut. Footsteps came down the passage very slowly. Then they stopped.

"In here, dear!" Mrs. Trapp called. "Dear," after what she'd been saying about her. People are hypocrites.

The girl came into the kitchen. She did not smile or say anything, but just looked at us. She really had the most expressionless face I had ever seen. It might have been carved out of wood. She must have something to hide, I thought.

"Sit down there, dear," Mrs. Trapp said, pointing to a chair. "Here you are. You tuck into that." She put a plate of sandwiches in front of the girl.

"Ta."

"Well, it's nice to see you've got manners. Your mum brought you up proper, didn't she?"

The girl did not answer. She sat eating her sandwich, and her eyes were all over the place, looking at the saucepans on the shelf, the calendar on the wall, the stove, the fridge. . . . Casing the joint, I thought.

"What's your mother's name, dear?" Mrs. Trapp asked.

"Louise."

"Louise what?"

"Martin."

"Louise Martin, now that's a pretty name," Mrs. Trapp said, trying to soften her up. "And how old are you?"

"Thirteen."

"When's your birthday?" I asked quickly.

She looked at me. She had answered Mrs. Trapp's questions readily enough, but she obviously resented mine. I got the impression that she did not like me. When it comes to that, I didn't like her either.

"What's it got to do with you? Gonna give me a present, are you?" she asked sarcastically.

"Now that's enough of that," Mrs. Trapp said sharply. "I'm not having any of that in my kitchen, thank you."

The girl and I looked at her, and then back at each other. For the first time, a brief spark of fellow feeling passed between us. I don't mean we were friends; it was just the look one exchanges when grown-ups say something particularly silly. Any of what, for heaven's sake?

"And where do you come from?" Mrs. Trapp asked. "Where's your home?"

"Still where I left it, I hope," the girl said pertly, and looked at me again, as if inviting me onto her side. I looked away quickly. I was with Mrs. Trapp. I wasn't with her. I felt excited. It was like a game. Mrs. Trapp and I were the detectives and she was the suspect. We weren't horrid to her, we only asked her questions. Mrs. Trapp called her dear, and I poured her out some more milk and the sun shone in through the window. We were enjoying ourselves, like cats stalking a bird. Somehow I felt a bit ashamed of it later. There were two of us and only one of her. She was quite alone.

I had been sure that my father would know immediately what to do. People were always saying to me in front of him what a clever father I had, and although he would shake his head modestly, I could tell he secretly agreed with them. So I was astonished to hear him say, "You mustn't let sentiment blind you, Margaret. This is a very tricky situation. It's important that we shouldn't commit ourselves until I've had time to consider it more fully. It's not easy, not easy at all."

He was in the sitting room talking to my mother. They had left the door ajar, which was silly of them if they did not want to be overheard. Anyone could have been outside in the hall. They were lucky it was only me. Not that I had meant to eavesdrop, for I had not heard my father come in. It was merely surprise that stopped me, just out of sight, with the cup of coffee I had been bringing my mother still in my hand.

"She must be Emma," my mother said. She sounded exhausted, as if she had cried herself dry. I imagined her looking gray and creased, like the sand when the sea has gone out. "Who else could she be? I can't believe any mother would do that to her own child."

"I'm afraid, Margaret, you haven't got my experience of human nature," my father said. "You've no idea what people will do, if they think there's money in it. Personally, I find this letter very suspect."

"I thought it was a sad letter," my mother said, in her vague, tired voice. "Didn't you think it was sad, Anthony?"

"Oh, very touching," my father said. I could imagine his left eyebrow going up, as if asking my mother how she could be so gullible. "I'm sure it was carefully calculated to rend our heartstrings. Look at those tearstains. A little overdone, don't you think? One or two she might have got away with, but this looks as if she's used a watering can. And then, to cap it all, she sends the girl to us on the first of August—she was probably very proud of that touch. But have you asked yourself, Margaret, how she knew it was Emma's birthday? The papers didn't give the date."

"I don't know. I can only think of that poor child and how she will feel. . . . It doesn't seem to matter who she is, whether she is Emma or not . . ."

"On the contrary, it matters very much," my father said sharply.

My mother was silent.

"You're sure the girl doesn't know what is in the letter?" my father asked.

"She said not. And I didn't tell her. I didn't know how to."

"Good. And I asked Mrs. Trapp not to, so—by the way, where's Kate?"

He had remembered me at last. Already I was coming second to the girl in his mind.

My mother said she thought I was in the kitchen with Mrs. Trapp and Rosie. This was my cue to come forward with the cup of coffee, but I hesitated too long.

"Good Lord! I trust you didn't tell Kate what was in the letter?"

"I . . . it was such a shock. I felt dizzy. I can't remember what I said."

"You didn't leave the letter lying about?"

"I think I must have dropped it."

"She's read it then," my father said. Something in his voice really hurt me. It sounded so cold and weary, as if I had worn out his love a long time ago, and there was nothing left. "And I've no doubt she will have told . . ."

I did not wait to hear any more.

"Mummy?" I called in a small voice, trying to make it sound as if I were only halfway across the hall instead of right outside the door.

"We're in here, Kate."

I waited a second or two and then pushed the door wide. "I've brought you some . . . Oh, Daddy!" I exclaimed with affected surprise. "I didn't hear you come in."

Perhaps I overdid it. His eyebrow went up. He looked at me and then at the cup of coffee in my hand. To my dismay I saw the milk had already formed a wrinkled skin across the top. But all he said was, "I should give that to your mother while it's still lukewarm. I'm glad you're here, Kate. I want to ask you something and I want you to answer me truthfully."

"Yes, of course."

"There's no 'of course' about it," he said. "Trust has to be earned, Kate. It's not given away free in packets of cornflakes. Have you read this letter?" The bright blue paper was in his hand.

"Yes," I said. There seemed little point in saying no. "Mummy fainted and I thought . . ."

"Never mind the excuses. Have you told the girl—ah—Rosie, what was in the letter?"

"No."

"No?"

"Honestly, Daddy. I haven't."

He looked at me thoughtfully and then said, "Why not?"

The question confused me. His questions often did. You never knew where they were going to hit you.

"Come on, Kate, answer quickly. Don't try to . . ."

"Anthony, you're not in court now. Does it matter?"

"The truth always matters, Margaret," he said stiffly. "Naturally I'm interested in Kate's reaction."

"It's hardly evidence. I don't think a judge would be impressed by a child's failing to recognize someone she's never seen, do you?"

"Don't be ridiculous, Margaret," my father said. His face looked wooden, as it always does when he is trying not to lose his temper. I wondered why he was suddenly angry—not even with me but with my mother. They had been speaking quietly but the air seemed full of disturbance, as if the sound waves were all tangled. I looked from one to the other, puzzled. They hardly ever quarreled in front of me; at least not when they knew I was there. It's all *her* fault, I thought. That girl's.

"She isn't Emma, Daddy, she isn't. I'm sure she isn't," I said quickly.

"As your mother kindly pointed out, Kate, you're

hardly in a position to know," he said. But I could tell my words had pleased him. For some reason, he did not want the girl to be Emma.

I suppose I should have been glad to find him on my side. I don't know why I felt uneasy. Perhaps it was the scent of lavender coming in through the open window. I had always hated the scent of lavender.

"Her name's Rosie and she's horrible!" I said.

5

There is a certain piercing sound that my father cannot stand, such as the noise I make when I lose my temper.

"You sound like a fishwife," he used to say.

When I was small, I thought he meant a female fish, which puzzled me, for however hard I pressed my ear against my aquarium, I could hear nothing, though I could see my goldfish opening and shutting their mouths as if they were screaming soundlessly. When I learned that fishwives were women famous only for their shrill, scolding voices, I was hurt.

Rosie outclassed me completely. No fishwife would have stood a chance against her. I have never heard anyone shout and scream and swear as loudly as she did when she found out what was in her mother's letter.

My father had not meant to tell her, not at first.

"There's no point in upsetting her until we have had time to make some investigations," he said. At that time he had not met Rosie and had no idea what he was up against. "Leave it to me, Margaret."

He had wanted to see Rosie alone, but for once my mother was obstinate.

"I want to be there," she said. "I can't hide away for ever."

"It was very sensible of you to wait till I came, Margaret," my father told her. "You know you're inclined to be emotional. It would have been all too easy to say the wrong thing."

"Such as 'Welcome home, Emma'?" my mother asked.

"I've yet to be convinced she is Emma," he said coldly. "Well, come along. We'd better not keep her waiting any longer. No, Kate, not you. You stay here."

"That's not fair! Why can't I come? It's as much to do with me as anyone."

He hesitated, and then shrugged. I think he knew there was no way of making me stay put, unless he tied me to a chair. I followed them to the kitchen.

Mrs. Trapp looked relieved to see us. I think Rosie must have been annoying her. "Here's Mr. Seton now," she said. "I told you he wouldn't be long."

"Not half," the girl muttered, and Mrs. Trapp said sharply, "You mind your manners."

"Thank you, Mrs. Trapp," my father said. "You've been very kind. I appreciate it. But now I'm sure you must be anxious to get home."

He had no success with her either. Like me, Mrs. Trapp was determined to see what happened. She was in no hurry, she said, and wouldn't dream of leaving dear Mrs. Seton when she was so poorly. "You sit down, dear," she told my mother. "You've had a shock, and with your poor nerves you want to be careful."

"There's really no need . . ." my father began. I don't know how this little battle would have ended, because the girl interrupted it, saying in a bored voice, "If you got my answer, mister, I'll be off."

My father looked at her. Though he smiled, his eyes were sharp.

"Ah, Rosie," he said. "Rosie—I'm afraid I don't know your surname?"

"Martin."

"Rosie Martin. We must have a little talk. Perhaps we can go into my study . . ."

"Ain't you even wrote it yet?" the girl demanded indignantly. "I been waiting ages."

"I'm sorry about that. I came as quickly as I could."

"The letter wasn't addressed to you," the girl pointed out. "Mrs. it said on the envelope. Not Mr. Why couldn't *she* answer it? Instead of keeping me hanging about all day."

"Well, that's gratitude for you," Mrs. Trapp said indignantly. "You had a good lunch, my girl. Better than you get at home, I shouldn't be surprised."

"No, it ain't then."

"Please!" my father said sharply, and they were both quiet, looking at him. "Mrs. Trapp, since you're staying, perhaps you could make us all some tea. Rosie, I'm afraid this may come as a surprise to you." He was watching her carefully, but if he hoped to judge anything by her expression, he was out of luck. Her face was at its most wooden. "Your mother wrote that she has had to go away for a time, and has asked us to look after you."

"Go away?" the girl repeated blankly. "What d'you mean? She didn't say nothing to me about going away. And why can't I stay at home like I always done before? I don't want to stay here. I mean, ta and all that, but— but I ain't even got my nightie," she ended triumphantly, as if that settled it.

My father smiled. "I expect Kate can lend you one," he began, but she was no longer listening to him.

"Had to go away," she repeated slowly. "How d'you mean, *had* to go away?" She looked quickly at Mrs. Trapp and then back at my father. "*She* said you was a lawyer. Mum don't want a lawyer. She ain't done nothing wrong. 'Oo's been telling you lies? Mum ain't done nothing." Her voice was rising now, like a whistling kettle.

Everyone except me started saying soothing things —"No, no, of course not." "You misunderstand me," and so on. She took no notice. She was on her feet now, her eyes darting around suspiciously.

"Where's Mum? I want my mum. What've they done with her? They ain't put her in prison, have they?"

"No, my dear."

Her face went the color of bacon fat. "She ain't . . . ?"

"No," my mother said quickly. "I'm sure she's all right, my dear. You mustn't worry."

"Where is she, then?" Rosie demanded, and when we all hesitated, not knowing the answer to that, she began to shout at us, swearing and calling us liars and nutters and a lot of other names I did not understand. My mother tried to put her arm round her, but she hit it away. That made me furious and I began to shout too. Mrs. Trapp began to shout at both of us and my mother began to cry. It was then my father took the blue letter out of his pocket and gave it to Rosie.

"Perhaps you had better read your mother's letter," he said.

Now we were all silent, watching her. The little noises came into their own again; the fridge humming, a fly hitting against the window as it tried to find its way out, the blue paper rustling in the girl's hand. She read quickly, her head moving slightly from side to side, her blue eyelids reflecting the bright color of the letter. Her hand was not quite steady, I noticed. She turned the sheet over and read the postscript before she spoke. Then she only muttered, " 'Oo's bleeding baby? What's she on about?" and started to read it from the beginning again.

None of us spoke. I glanced at my father and thought he looked as if he regretted having given her the letter.

"Of course," he said, just before she had finished reading for the second time, "it's probably all a misunderstanding."

It was then she exploded. We had not wanted her (at least my father and I did not. I don't know about my mother). Now she made it very plain, at the top of her voice so that the whole of Hampstead could hear, that she did not want us.

"I hate you!" she screamed. "I hate you!"

6

A sort of washed-out peace descended on our house after Rosie and my father had gone. He was driving her to her home, to see if they could find out where her mother was. They did not live in a flat, she told us, but in a room at Number 14 Strinton Road, Hockley (a rough part of London, Mrs. Trapp informed me later). They were not on the telephone, although Rosie had given my father the number of a friend two doors down, who, she said, would take messages in an emergency. But when my father tried the number, there was no reply.

"She'll be at bingo, I bet," Rosie had said. She was

more cheerful now that my father had offered to drive her home. "That a Rolls?" she'd asked hopefully when she saw his car in the drive.

"No, I'm sorry. Only a Daimler."

My mother had wanted to go with them, but Rosie had said rudely, "No. Don't let her come." She seemed nervous of my mother and kept out of her reach. I think she was afraid that if Mummy kissed her (as she probably would have done, given half a chance), it would be like a stamp on a legal document, signing, sealing, and delivering her over to us for ever.

I had stepped forward then, but she'd glanced at me with her hard gray eyes and said quickly, "I don't want her neither."

"That's good, because I don't want you!" I'd shouted angrily, and my father had frowned at me before he drove off. It wasn't fair. She was allowed to be rude and nobody told her off. I was the one who was blamed. I think I saw then how it would always be if she came back. And I hoped she never would.

We had a long wait. Mrs. Trapp made us tea and toast, and settled herself comfortably into a chair next to my mother.

"You poor dear, you'll feel better with something inside you," she said. Her voice was hushed with sympathy, as if she was at a funeral, but her eyes were bright. I knew she was dying to gossip, and so was I. "What a thing to happen . . ."

But my mother had her own way of dealing with us.

"You've been so kind," she said in a faint voice, putting her hand over her eyes to shut out our eager faces. "I've such a terrible headache. I think I'll follow your advice, Mrs. Trapp, and try and rest quietly for a time."

Mrs. Trapp swallowed her disappointment nobly. She really is kind and was fond of my mother. She drew the curtains to keep the sun out of the room, and tip-toed out, beckoning me to follow.

"Poor thing, it's all been too much for her," she said.

I nodded. Rosie was too much for me too.

"I expect that girl's mother is at home all the time. Mr. Seton will know how to deal with her."

"Yes."

"I wonder what your dad will do if she isn't, though."

"I don't know. I expect he'll find someone he can leave Rosie with."

Mrs. Trapp looked a little shocked at that. "He can't just dump her, dear. I mean, supposing she is your . . ."

"She isn't. She isn't."

"Shh, dear. You'll wake your mother. No, I don't think she is for a moment. Common little thing, did you hear her language? Still, I suppose if she's been brought up different . . ."

"She's nothing like us!"

Mrs. Trapp nodded her head in agreement. "That's true enough," she said. "She doesn't take after any of you. I had a good look at her while we were waiting, and I thought to myself, she's never a Seton. And she certainly doesn't take after your mother's side, not with that dark hair. No, dear, you're quite right. It must be a trick. I wonder if your mother'd like me to make up a bed in case she comes back."

"She won't be coming back."

Mrs. Trapp looked at me curiously. I thought there was disapproval in her gaze and flushed. "Now, you don't want to be jealous, dear," she said. "Your mum and dad love you best, stands to reason."

"I'm not jealous. It's just that she's not Emma. She isn't. If it was Emma, I'd love her. I'd want her."

"Yes, of course," Mrs. Trapp said soothingly. "Still, she's a human being, after all. A child. You can't help feeling sorry for her, can you? I expect that's how your mum and dad feel, just sorry for her." She looked at me slyly. "You've always been a kindhearted little girl, Kate. I mean, look how you love animals. I'm sure you'll be ever so kind to her if she does come back."

This is one of the ways grown-ups tell lies. Mrs. Trapp was far from sure that I would be kind to Rosie. She was just warning me that I had better be, if I didn't want to put myself in the wrong.

"I've always wondered about that Bible story," she went on. "You know, the one about the prodigal son. I bet his brother wasn't best pleased when he came back and his father made such a fuss over him, killing them fatted calves for his supper. Still, it's human nature, I suppose."

Though I didn't answer, I took Mrs. Trapp's warning to heart. I helped her make up the bed in the room next to mine. I put my second-best nightie on the pillow and my second-best teddy beside it. Mrs. Trapp told me I was a good, kind girl, and I tried to make my face as wooden as Rosie's so that she could not guess the fury I felt inside.

This was the room that should have been Emma's. This was the bed Emma should have slept in. Often I had lain on it, dreaming of my sister. I could picture her clearly in my mind even now. She had straight fair hair like mine. Her eyes were round and blue-gray, like mine. There was a little gap between her front teeth so that she lisped a little as she said, "Tell me another thtory, Kate." Somehow in my dreams she was always small, so that she had to look up to me. Silly, really, when all the time I knew she was two years older than me.

I had loved her, this little lost sister. I wasn't going to let Rosie take her place.

It was late when they came back. Mrs. Trapp had left, reluctantly, some hours ago. My mother had already had time to worry in case there had been an accident, and to reassure herself that it was bound to take time. Mrs. Martin might not be there and my father would have to make inquiries. . . . I too had begun to worry, although I did not let my mother know, not wanting to upset her. I thought of all sorts of horrible things, that they had kidnapped my father, or robbed and killed him. We were both relieved when at last we heard the sound of the car, and rushed out into the hall.

Rosie came in first, with my father behind her. The picture of her I had been building up, of a sly, malevolent creature, vanished from my mind.

She did not look the same girl. All the fight had gone out of her; even her dark spiky hair now fell limply over her forehead, and she seemed to have shrunk. She stood there, clutching three carrier-bags so tightly that her knuckles stood out like knobbly white buttons. Her face was more wooden than ever, and she was looking, not at us, but down at the floor, so that her blue eyelids seemed to gaze out like blind eyes.

My mother said softly, "Hullo, Rosie. I'm glad you're back." She glanced inquiringly at my father, who shook his head. They had not found the mother.

I did not say anything. I could not. I'm not actually as horrible as I make out. All I felt at that moment was pity. I would have rushed forward and hugged her and said "Welcome home, Emma" if I'd thought that it would take that frozen look off her face. But I did not. She was like a strange stray dog that has wandered into your house, and you're sorry for it but afraid to pet it in case it bites.

"You must be hungry," my mother was saying. "Supper won't be long. Perhaps you'd like to take your things up to your room first. Shall I show you the way?"

Rosie's eyes lifted a little but only as far as my mother's waist, and she did not say anything. I thought she was still nervous of my mother, so I said quickly, "I'll take Rosie up. You get supper, Mummy. I'm starving."

My mother looked at me a little doubtfully. "Would you like Kate to go with you, Rosie?" she asked.

The girl nodded, still without looking at any of us. "Yeh. Ta," she muttered.

So we went upstairs together, Rosie and I. Her carrier-bags bumped against her knees, but when I asked her if I could carry one for her, she shook her head and clutched them even more tightly, as if her whole life was in them and she was afraid to let it go.

I was glad Mrs. Trapp and I had made the room look so nice. We had put roses on the dressing table, to go with the roses on the curtains, and turned the sheet back on the bed so that it would look welcoming. My second-best teddy bear sat smiling on the pillow.

"His name's William," I said. "I expect you're too old for toys really, like me, but they sort of make a room look cozy."

"Yeh. Ta."

"I hope my nightie will fit you. You're taller than me but I'm fatter, so it ought to be all right."

"Yeh. Ta."

She was still clutching her carrier-bags as if she didn't know what to do with them.

"We've cleared the top drawer out," I said, opening it to show her. "You can put your things in here if you like."

"Ta."

"It's quite a nice room, isn't it? Look, you can see the garden from the window." I was like an estate agent, showing off a house to a client who didn't like it and wasn't going to buy it, but was too polite to say so.

Rosie did glance briefly out of the window.

"Yeh," she said. There was an awkward pause, for I had run out of ideas. Then, as if she knew it was her turn, she added, "Big, innit?"

"Yes," I agreed gratefully. "It's a third of an acre. That's jolly good for London, isn't it?"

"Yeh."

I suddenly felt like crying. I wanted to be kind but I did not know how to be. I felt shy and stiff. There were so many questions I'd have liked to ask her, but I was afraid of upsetting her—and getting blamed for it.

"You got a telly?" she asked suddenly.

"Yes." I was about to say we'd got two, but was afraid it would sound like boasting. "Yes, there's one in my playroom. Would you like to watch it?"

"Yeh. I don't mind," she said.

So we went and sat in front of the television in my playroom. I think it was a relief to both of us. We did not have to speak. When I glanced at her out of the corner of my eye from time to time, she was staring at the set, but somehow I felt she did not even see it. There was a comic on, doing all sorts of silly things, some of them quite funny, but I never saw her smile once. I wondered what pictures she was seeing in her mind instead.

Somehow I began to feel frightened, sitting watching the bright picture in the darkening room. It was as if strange horrors were seeping out of Rosie's head into mine. I saw us all suddenly as we must appear to her, rich and smug, smiling falsely at her, as brightly colored as the little figures on the screen, and as cold to touch. I felt any moment she would reach out and turn a knob, and we would vanish. I was glad when my mother called us down to supper.

7

After supper my father said firmly, "You must be tired," and sent us both to bed. I didn't argue, although it was only nine o'clock, as I was planning to come down again as soon as Rosie was safely in her room. But my mother guessed, and when she came up to kiss me good-night, she said, "I want you to promise to stay in bed. Please, Kate. No creeping downstairs. No listening at doors."

"I don't . . ." I began, but it was no good. I had been caught too often. My mother merely had to look at me and I felt myself flushing. "Well, I wouldn't have to, if you told me things. You never tell me anything. It's not fair. *She* knows what happened. She was there. And I bet Daddy's told you. Why should I always be left out?"

"Darling, you're not," she said quickly, and sitting down on my bed, took my hand in hers. "It's just that there isn't much to tell. She'd already packed up and gone, this Mrs. Martin, I mean, leaving Rosie's carrier-bags in the middle of the floor. There was no note, not even a message. And none of the other people in the house knew where she'd gone. In fact, she hadn't told anyone she was leaving."

"Not even the landlady?"

"Especially not the landlady, I gather."

"You mean she left without paying the rent?"

"Now, Kate, I didn't say that," she said hastily, and refused to talk about it anymore, saying that she had told me all she knew. "Please, Kate, I've had all I can stand." Her voice rose in the way that always frightened me. I hated it when she cried. But she took a deep breath and added more quietly, "We don't want Rosie to think we're discussing her behind her back, do we?"

She'd have to be pretty dumb if she didn't guess, I thought, but I did not say it aloud. At times I think Miss Wait would be quite surprised how nice I am, even though I'm only a child.

My mother had left my door ajar, as she always did, so that the landing light would shine into my room. Not that I'm frightened of the dark now, but I used to be, and it created a precedent, as my father would say. I heard her open Rosie's door quietly. Silence. Then she said in a low voice, "Good night, my dear. Sleep well." No answer. My mother closed the door softly and went downstairs.

I could not get to sleep. Bits of the day kept tossing and turning in my head, showing different pictures, all of them of Rosie. Her face kept changing. First it was hard and insolent, then a screaming, childish face, spitting out desperate accusations: "It's a lie. Mum never wrote that. You done it yourself. It's all lies." Then a third face, pinched and pathetic, the face of a homeless waif, too timid to meet your eyes, too frightened to speak above a mumble.

These three faces floated against my closed lids like colored balloons in a dark sky. I tried to bring them together into one face, the true face of Rosie Martin, but they kept slipping away.

I opened my eyes and lay staring at the crack of light coming through my door. I heard the wind in the garden and the distant sound of traffic on the road. I heard my parents coming up to bed, walking quietly so as not to wake me. Then I listened to the silence in the room next to mine.

It wasn't the silence of an empty room. It was more positive than that, as if someone inside was holding her breath, and waiting. Perhaps she was lying in bed with her eyes wide open too. Perhaps we were both listening to each other's silence.

"Your parents didn't ought to let her stay in the house tonight," Mrs. Trapp had said. "Or she'll be sneaking down when you're asleep, and letting them in."

Now the night seemed full of noises. Whispering in the garden outside, false owls exchanging signals in the dark, floorboards creaking. . . . I was just telling myself it was all imagination, when I heard, quite distinctly, footsteps in the passage outside my room.

Hardly daring to breathe, I stared at the half-open door. All I could see in the dim light of the landing was a slice of carpet and two banisters. A figure briefly blotted these out and was gone. It was Rosie. Rosie in my second-best nightie, creeping downstairs to let them in. Them. The robbers.

I got silently out of bed, tiptoed across the landing, and looked over the banisters. She had reached the bottom step. I waited for her to go to the front door, open it, and set the burglar alarm screaming the night awake. Serve her right, I thought with satisfaction. Her friends will run off and she will go with them, and I'll never see her or my second-best nightie again.

To my surprise, she did not go to the door but turned into the shadowed part of the hall. I leaned farther over the banisters. Now I could only see a pale shape in the darkness. She seemed to be standing in the middle of the hall. Listening, perhaps. Then she walked silently to the left-hand wall. The telephone!

She began to dial. I had no time to warn her, even if I'd wanted to, that there was an extension in my father's room that pinged every time you dialed a number downstairs. I stood on the landing and waited.

He must have opened his door very quietly, for I did not hear it. He suddenly appeared, wearing his dressing gown, with his hair rumpled and his feet bare. A look of exasperation came over his face when he saw I was there before him. I opened my mouth, but he shook his head and held up a finger to quiet me. Then, after he had glanced over the banisters into the hall below, he took my arm and led me back into my room, pushing the door gently shut behind him.

"Do you know whom she's phoning?" he asked in a low voice.

"No."

"Did she ask you if she could use the phone?"

"No."

"But you knew she was going to?"

"No. I heard her go by."

He was silent for a moment. Then he whispered, "Stay here," and went out onto the landing. I counted five and then followed him. Fortunately his back was towards me, because he had not gone downstairs as I had expected, but was looking over the banisters and listening. I listened too, but could hear nothing. I imagined Rosie leaning against the wall in the dark, hearing a telephone ringing, ringing in an empty room. But whose room?

Now my father moved over to the double switch by the head of the stairs and put his hand out. A brilliant light flooded the hall below. Rosie swung round and dropped the receiver. She looked terrified.

"Hullo, my dear," my father said, going down the stairs towards her. "Isn't it a bit late to be making a telephone call?"

She did not answer. I think she was too frightened to.

"Whom were you trying to ring?"

"Nobody."

"Nobody?"

"Just a friend."

"Really? At half-past one in the morning?"

I hated his voice when he talked in this way, with a kind of teasing mockery. When he spoke to me like that, it always made me feel small and stupid and furious. It made me angry now.

"I expect she didn't realize it was so late," I said loudly, leaning over the banisters. "I expect her watch has stopped. They often do, when you move house, you know."

My father looked up at me. After a brief pause, he said dryly, "No, I didn't know. Thank you for telling me, Kate. Was that it, Rosie?"

"Yeh," she muttered, then added with a rush, "I thought my friend might know where Mum's gone. But he didn't answer."

"He's probably asleep," my father said. "Sensible boy. I suggest we follow his example. You're welcome to use the telephone in the morning, Rosie. You have only to ask. But not late at night, please. There's an extension by my bed that makes a noise when you dial down here, and I'm a very light sleeper."

"Sorry," she said, and dodging round him nervously, came running up the stairs. As she passed me, her eyes met mine and she whispered, "I ain't got no watch. Ta all the same, kid."

Somehow it made me cross, the careless way she said it, as if she took my support for granted. Who did she think she was?

After her door had shut behind her, I looked once more over the banisters. My father was standing in the middle of the hall. His back was towards me. I could not see the expression on his face. But I heard him say gently under his breath, "Poor child."

He was talking about her, not me.

The owls were still hooting when I went back to bed, but they were not the birds in my mind. I was thinking about cuckoos. The cuckoo lays her egg in another bird's nest and flies away. And when the egg hatches, the young cuckoo grows bigger and bigger, until one day it pushes the true fledgling right out of the nest.

8

Rosie Martin was clever. I knew this the moment I looked out of my window in the morning. She was already up, sitting on my swing in the garden below, rocking idly backwards and forwards, a half-eaten apple in one hand. This was a fourth Rosie she was presenting to us, a young and innocent Rosie, wearing a white T-shirt, denim shorts, and yellow flip-flops on her bare feet. The wind had ruffled her dark hair, so that it no longer hung stiff as a portcullis above her eyes. Though I could not be sure from this distance, I would have bet (and won my bet), that she was no longer wearing makeup.

She looked very much at home in my garden. Like a chameleon, she was assuming the color of her surroundings. You could easily have taken her for the daughter of the house.

Now my father came out and crossed the grass towards her. He said something I could not hear, and she smiled up at him and got off the swing. They turned and walked back to the house together. My father was looking down at her kindly, indulgently; very differently from the way he looks at me.

It was then I decided to search her room.

All right, you can say I was mean and jealous. But someone had to be sensible. My mother was already won over (no difficult task), and now my father was softening, both in his heart and his brain too, if you ask me. And I knew Mrs. Trapp would blow round the compass to anyone's breath. There was only me left.

I could hear my mother and Mrs. Trapp talking in the kitchen downstairs. No noise from my father's study, but the door was thick. He was in there with Rosie, asking her the questions he had been too tactful to ask her last night—who are your mother's friends? Employers? Can you think of anywhere she might have gone? That should keep them busy.

I went into Rosie's room. There was hardly a trace of her there; no photographs propped up on the dressing table, no knickknacks on top of the chest of drawers. She had even made the bed, so that the room looked as it had always done, except for a blue parka hanging behind the door, and my second-best teddy on the chair by the bed.

The top drawer of the chest, the one I had told her she could use, was half empty. Was this all she had? A few folded clothes, shabby but clean, toothbrush and makeup, brush and comb, school books . . . I glanced into these and saw that she was good at math and French and geography, getting better marks than I ever did, which didn't please me.

There was nothing to prove who she was. No birth certificate. No photographs. No letters. Only an old Valentine card, claiming she was the true sweetheart of a boy named Tim, but that didn't help.

I shut the drawer and looked round the room, frowning. It wasn't natural, was it? I mean, to have lived for thirteen years and to have so little to show for it. She must be hiding something. One day, I'd find out what.

That was the first bad thing I did, searching her room. The second was worse. I wouldn't have done it if I hadn't heard that fat hypocrite in her blue overall and yellow rubber gloves (Mrs. Trapp, I mean), telling my mother what a sweet girl Rosie was, and how you could tell there was good breeding there somewhere.

"I know she doesn't look like any of you now," she said. "But feed her up a bit and, well, really, except for her being dark and those eyes, I mean there won't be much difference, will there?"

"No," I said sarcastically. "We've all got two eyes, two arms, and two legs. I wonder how you'll tell us apart."

"Kate!" my mother said reproachfully.

Neither of them seemed very pleased to see me. They had obviously been having a lovely time in the kitchen, cooking Rosie into Emma as fast as they could, probably planning shopping expeditions and choosing a suitable school for her. They were playing with their new toy and had no time for me.

I went back upstairs, and as I passed the bookcase on the landing I remembered my father's old family album. I took it out, carried it into my room, and opened it.

My great-grandfather was in here, and my grandfather, both of whom had died before I was born. Faded brown photographs of young men with mustaches, old men with gray beards. There was my grandmother as a young woman, her chest already curving like a pigeon's, her hair in a curly fringe (nothing like Rosie's). On her lap, in a long white christening gown, lay my baby father, with eyes like buttons and no nose worth mentioning. Now my father as a gap-toothed boy, grinning widely at the camera, and holding a cricket bat, or linking arms with his younger brother, my uncle James. It's strange. Looking at grown-ups, it's impossible to imagine them as children, yet in these old photographs I recognized them immediately. Uncle Rob. Aunt Patricia. There was even a square girl with thin plaits and thick legs who was unmistakably Miss Wait. And there were cousins, not all of whom I knew. My father has too many cousins to remember. Boys playing on the beach, rowing on a river, riding over the downs. How happy my father looked, how carefree. I wondered what I would have thought of him if I had known him then, as a curly-haired boy no older than myself. Perhaps we would have been friends.

I had forgotten what I was looking for and almost missed it, having to turn back two pages for another look. It was a photograph of three boys. My father was in the center, Uncle James on the right, and a dark-haired boy on the left. It was the dark-haired boy at whom I looked.

No, I thought, relieved. It isn't like Rosie. Not really. His face is wider, his chin more square, his nose bigger. It's nothing like her at all. It's just the dark hair.

I turned on again, but the likeness I had half seen haunted me, and in the end I had to turn back. The photograph showed only their heads and shoulders, but I thought they must have been standing on a beach, because there was nothing behind them but sky. A wind was blowing the boy's dark hair so that it fell forward over his eyes in spikes. But the face was different, quite different, nothing like Rosie's.

I slipped the photograph out of the corners that held it, and turned it over. On the back was written in a schoolboy's hand (Uncle James's it must have been), "Me and Anthony and our cousin Robbie at Hastings." Robbie. I had never heard of him.

I turned it round and studied it again. Then I put my finger over the lower part of the face, and there it was, the fleeting resemblance that had caught my eye. It was nothing to do with his features or the shape of his head. It was merely the way the eyes stared out boldly from beneath straight black brows. That was all there was to it, a chance expression and the wind-blown hair.

I tore the photograph into tiny pieces and flushed it down the lavatory. The moment the water swirled the fragments out of sight, I regretted it.

Back in my room, I sat on the bed and wished and wished I could put the clock back, the photograph back, or that I had never touched the album at all. More than anything I wanted to study the face again, to reassure myself that it was nothing like Rosie's—the wrong shape, a wider mouth, a different chin. I looked through the rest of the album, but there were no more photographs of Robbie. I had destroyed his image. Already his face was fading in my memory, and into its place crept a thin, spiky girl with a pointed chin and bold eyes. There was no way I could get rid of her now.

I don't know what made me ring Miss Wait. I was feeling miserable and guilty and confused—perhaps I thought she would be on my side. I could imagine her taking one look at Rosie and saying "Of course she's an impostor. Children always impose on you if you give 'em half a chance." I should have remembered that Miss Wait never took sides, being too fond of making her own way straight down the middle, no matter whose toes she trod on.

I had been afraid she might be out walking her dogs, but she answered almost at once.

"Hullo? Who is it? Speak up."

"It's me. Kate."

My voice must have sounded odd, because she said immediately, "Kate, what's the matter?"

"Can you come and see us today?" I said. "Please."

"Yes, of course. Right away. What's happened? Is your mother ill?"

"No. It's . . . Emma's come back." The name slipped out. I had not meant to say it. I added quickly, "Only it's not Emma at all. It's not! It's Rosie. Rosie Martin."

"Take a deep breath and count up to five," Miss Wait advised. "And try not to snivel, you'll make the telephone wet and fuse it or something. That's better. Now tell me exactly what's happened."

I told her, and when I had finished, she said, "I'll come up at once. In fact, wild horses wouldn't keep me away. Expect me in an hour."

As I put the telephone down, I wondered uneasily if my parents would be pleased to see her.

9

We had lunch in the garden under the elderberry tree.

"Do we have to eat out here all the time?" my father demanded irritably, flicking away a wasp with his napkin. His early kindness seemed to have worn thin. I wondered what had happened to annoy him, and glanced at Rosie, hoping it was her fault. Her face was as inscrutable as ever.

"Did you have any luck?" my mother asked.

My father shook his head. "Saturday's a bad day, of course."

"Three of Mum's ladies were out," Rosie said. "Shopping, I expect."

"Ladies?" my mother repeated blankly.

"Mum helps out. Like your Mrs. Trapp. Does for four ladies, on different days, of course. Scrubs the floors, see?" she said, looking at me angrily, as if it were my fault. I didn't say anything. I didn't care what her mother did.

I was very quiet all through lunch. My mother thought I was sulking and kept sending me reproachful messages with her eyes. But unspoken criticism never worries me. I have learned how to deal with it.

"Why do you keep frowning, Mummy? Have you got a headache?" I asked.

After that, she left me in peace.

I was not sulking, as it happened. I was worrying about Miss Wait's arrival and how to avoid the blame for it. They were bound to find out it was my doing. Miss Wait was no woman for secrets. She would come striding in, saying in her loud, confident voice "Now what's all this Kate's been telling me?" And my father would glance at me with weary exasperation, as if I were the last straw and he wished the wind would blow me away. Everything I did was wrong, I thought. A deep depression descended on me. The sun seemed to shrink in the sky and the wind blew colder.

In my gloomy imagining, however, I hadn't allowed for the dog. It came bounding round the corner, a great grinning optimist of a dog, convinced against all reason that the whole world loved him. He covered the distance between us in three enormous leaps and flung himself on my father, leaving a trail of affectionate slobber on his lapel, and knocking two glasses off the table with one sweep of his plumed tail.

"Get down, you brute!" my father said angrily.

He shoved the dog away from him. Another glass fell from the table and broke.

"Look out, he'll cut his paws," I cried anxiously, and getting up, pushed the dog away from the broken glass—towards Rosie as it happened, though I swear it was not deliberate. She leapt up, knocking over her chair and screeching in terror.

"Keep him off! Keep him off of me!"

Perhaps mistaking her for a cat, the dog bounded happily towards her. She picked up the cheese from the table and threw it at him, then shinned up the elderberry tree like a monkey, disappearing into the green leaves.

"That's the last of the Stilton," my father said furiously.

It was then Miss Wait appeared round the corner.

"Ah, so that's where he's got to," she said cheerfully. "Here, Jasper! Come here, sir!"

The dog, transformed into an obedient retriever,

ran across the grass and deposited the half-eaten cheese at her feet.

"What's this you've got hold of?" she said. "Cheese? Really, Anthony, you should never feed dogs at the table. Terrible habit. Undoes months of training. And what's all this broken glass doing on the lawn?"

In the confusion of accusation and defense that followed, no one remembered me. I picked up the broken glass and then glanced up at the elderberry tree. Rosie's thin face was peering through the leaves.

"You can come down now," I said.

"I ain't coming down while that dog's loose."

"He won't hurt you. He's very friendly."

"Yeh. Like you."

"What do you mean?" I asked uneasily.

Before she could answer, Miss Wait caught sight of her.

"Hullo, who've you got hiding in that tree?" she asked. "Is this the girl? Come down and let's have a look at you, Emma or Rosie, whichever you are." I saw my parents exchange glances, each thinking the other must have told. "You're not frightened of dogs, are you? You can't be a Seton if you're afraid of dogs."

"I ain't a Seton. I'm Rosie Martin."

"Well, come down, Rosie Martin. You're giving me a crick in the neck."

"You gonna put that dog on the lead?"

"No need. He won't move unless I tell him to. STAY, JASPER!" she shouted as the dog was about to get up. He sank down again immediately and lay panting, his pink tongue lolling out of his mouth.

Rosie climbed doubtfully out of the tree.

"That's better. Now let's see," Miss Wait said, taking Rosie's chin in her hand. I expected Rosie to jerk her head away, but she seemed hypnotized, her eyes moving uneasily from Miss Wait to the dog and back again. "There've been plenty of dark Setons," Miss Wait went on, studying her thoughtfully, "I don't know. . . . Touch of Cousin Julia in that nose, do you think, Anthony? Let's see your profile, child. No. No, it's too straight. Julia's had a bump—though that might have been from falling off her pony, come to think of it. Caro was dark, but she was a hefty creature, like me. And that's not a Seton chin. Too pointed. Might come from your side, I suppose, Margaret? No. I can't give her a pedigree, I'm afraid."

"Don't want one," Rosie said angrily, and now she did jerk her head away. "I ain't a dog." She scowled at Miss Wait, who said, "The eyes. . . . Anthony, look, don't those eyes ring a bell? No, don't start smiling, child, frown as you did before. It's no good. It's gone. Why do children always get the giggles when you want them to be serious? What are you laughing at, Emma-Rose?"

"Dunno."

"Me, I expect," Miss Wait said, without rancor. She sat down at the table and helped herself to some biscuits. "Starving. Didn't have any lunch," she explained. "You might have left me some food, you pigs. Isn't there any cheese? Oh, I remember, you gave it to Jasper."

"I'll get you some, Elizabeth," my mother said quickly.

Miss Wait watched her out of sight, then turned to my father. "Come on, Anthony, tell all. You can't keep me out of this. Family affair. What are you going to do? I suppose you'll try and trace this—Mrs. Martin? Is there a Mr. Martin, by the way?" she added, turning to Rosie.

"He gone off," Rosie muttered, flushing.

"Do you remember him?"

"No."

"Were they married?"

Rosie turned furiously to my father. "I don't have to tell her, do I? What's it got to do with her? What's she poking her nose in for? 'Oo is she, anyway?"

My father began talking soothingly, but I don't think anyone listened to him. Miss Wait was staring at Rosie and frowning, though she seemed puzzled rather than cross. I glanced quickly at Rosie, and saw to my dismay that it was there again, the fleeting likeness to the photograph; the dark hair blowing across the forehead, the eyes staring out defiantly from beneath straight black brows.

"Now, who . . . ?" Miss Wait said slowly. I held my breath, terrified she would suddenly remember and say "Of course, Cousin Robbie!" and they would all go and look in the family album and find the empty space where his photograph should have been. But all she said was, "Whose eyes are those?"

"Mine," Rosie said defensively, as if she was being accused of theft. "They're mine. I ain't Emma."

Miss Wait looked at her curiously.

"What makes you so sure? Don't you want to be? Nice home, plenty of space, good family—what's so wrong with being Emma?"

"I want my own family," Rosie said. "I want my mum."

Miss Wait nodded, and turned to my father. "Loyal," she said. "I like that. Shows an affectionate nature. Very important in dogs and children. Where's Margaret with that cheese? Let's go and chase her up. The girls can stay here and make friends." She smiled at Rosie and added, "I'll take Jasper with me, though you'll have to get used to dogs if you're staying here."

"I ain't," Rosie said, but so softly that I don't think anybody heard her except me.

After they left us, we were silent. It was the first time we had been alone since yesterday, when we had sat in front of the television, each glad of an excuse not to speak. I glanced at her and found she had been watching me, although she looked away immediately. Her face was hard. If she had an affectionate nature, she certainly did not show it to me.

I wanted to say something friendly but the words would not come. I knew she despised me. She was part of the dangerous world outside, the world I saw through the windows of the car, as I was driven to and from school. She was part of the world that went shrieking and swearing over the heath outside our high garden wall, throwing over empty tins and stones and insults . . . "Take no notice, dear. They'll soon get tired of it." She was one of the children who hung about on street corners and jeered at us when we went past in our neat school single-file walk. One of them once snatched off my hat and threw it in the gutter—"Take no notice, Kate," the teacher said. "Don't answer back."

"Peasants," we called them in return. "Yobbos."

I knew I was one of the lucky ones. A good home, a good school. Great things were expected of me, great careers mine for the taking. . . . The trouble was, I knew I would muff it somehow. The prizes would slip between my fingers and leave me with nothing, and only myself to blame. Perhaps that was why I used to press my nose against the cold glass of the car window and look at the whooping children outside with envy.

"I wish I was poor and underprivileged," I told Mrs. Trapp once, but she told me not to be silly. I didn't know what I was talking about, she said.

"You know something?" Rosie asked suddenly.

"What?"

"We didn't ought to be enemies. We're on the same side. You want me out of here. I want me out of here too. Only I gotta find my mum first. You gonna help?"

"Yes. Yes, of course I will, Rosie," I said eagerly. Then added, "How?"

"Dunno yet, do I? You could cover for me if . . . but I suppose you'd go blabbing everything to your dad."

"No, I wouldn't," I promised, but I was puzzled. "Though I don't see why not. I mean, he wants to find her too."

"Yeh." She looked away from me, and began fiddling with a knife on the table. "Dunno that she'd like that. I mean, he's a lawyer and they got sort of fixed ideas, know what I mean? I don't want to get her into no trouble, see?"

"Yes," I agreed uncertainly. Was she implying her mother was some sort of a criminal? "I won't say anything, I promise, Rosie."

"Good kid," she said, and smiled at me. It was the first time I had seen her smile. Then her eyes shifted past me to the house. Turning, I saw my mother and Miss Wait standing just inside the French windows, looking out at us. Rosie got up and began to clear the lunch things onto the tray. "Meeting tonight," she said in a low voice. "In your room. After lights out, as they say on telly. Okay?"

"Yes."

I felt confused. It was a scene I had imagined so often happening with Emma. Emma and I giggling together when we were supposed to be asleep, making plans for the next day, telling stories. Only my Emma had had straight fair hair and round blue eyes. My dreams had not included anyone like Rosie.

10

Miss Wait said she had to give Jasper a run before driving back.

"You can come too, Kate," she said. "Do you good."

I was pleased, thinking she would tell me what they'd been talking about indoors. But she walked along in silence, her face as forbidding as a brick wall, and much the same color. Perhaps she was wondering whether to tell me anything at all. That's the trouble with having a bad reputation. People don't trust you. She probably thought I'd go blabbing to Rosie. I put on a secretive, trustworthy expression, but I don't think she noticed.

There was a wind on the heath. Children were flying kites. A fat man chased a newspaper over the dry grass. Every time he bent down to pick it up, it whisked out of his reach. I ran after it and returned it to him. "You're a kind girl," he said.

I went back to Miss Wait, who smiled and traced a halo round my head. Then she looked serious again and said, "I hope you are going to be kind."

"I've been very nice to her!"

"Oh, yes, to Rosie. . . . Actually I was thinking more about your parents. That wretched woman—she deserves to be shot! Dumping the child like left luggage —without any proof—it's too cruel."

"You don't think she's really Emma, do you?"

She spread her hands. "I've no idea. She could be."

"Daddy doesn't think she is."

She looked at me, raising her eyebrows. "Did he

really tell you that or are you just guessing? Guessing, I expect."

"He doesn't want her to be. I know he doesn't."

"No, you don't," she said firmly. "You don't know anything of the sort. Use your head, Kate. Naturally he wants to make sure. It would be too awful if they accepted her and it turned out to be a pack of lies. The woman could change her mind and want the child back —I wouldn't put anything past her. Or even worse, the child might run off again without a word. . . . It doesn't bear thinking of." She was silent for a moment, staring bleakly over the heath. I had never seen her look so grim. "Poor Anthony," she said at last. "To be put through all that again, it's too much. As if he hadn't suffered enough."

"It's Mummy I'm sorry for," I said.

"Well, yes, your mother too, of course. Though to be frank, I think it must be easier to have a nervous breakdown and lie in bed crying than to be the strong one who's got to carry on."

"That's not fair!" I cried hotly. "Mummy can't help being ill. It's easier for Daddy. He doesn't feel things as much as she does."

"Don't be so *stupid!*"

She was really angry and walked on quickly. I stayed where I was, tempted to shout after her that she was a fat ugly pig and I hated her. I probably would have done this a year ago, but I was more sensible now. I contented myself with muttering a few words I had learned from Rosie, causing two old ladies to look at me with shocked disapproval. Then I ran after her.

She had stopped some way ahead and was watching Jasper. The golden pedigree dog was playing happily with a spiky black mongrel. I wondered what she was thinking and thought I could guess—me and Rosie

—what a pity children weren't more like dogs. When I joined her, she did not look up. She was still cross with me.

"I didn't mean—" I began, but could not think of an end to my sentence.

"You shouldn't think that because people don't make a parade of their feelings it means they haven't got any," she said. "I know self-control has gone out of fashion, but if you ask me, it's a pity."

I was stung, feeling I had controlled myself pretty well only a minute ago, but I did not say anything.

"I suppose it's not really your fault," she went on, taking a look at my sulky face. "You never knew your father before it happened. He was very different then. Well, I suppose we all have to change. He was a sensitive boy, you know. Didn't even like hunting. I remember once when I was staying with them, he told your grandfather he felt sorry for the fox." She gave a bark of laughter. "That took courage, believe me. 'You've yet to convince me that the fox really enjoys it, Father,' he said, cool as a cucumber. I had to laugh, and that didn't improve matters, as you can imagine. We were both sent from the room. Still, we had some good times in those days."

I remembered the old photographs of my father as a laughing boy. It was all so long ago.

"What was Mummy like then?" I asked.

"I only met her later, when they got engaged. She was a pretty girl. Fond of parties and new clothes. She'd been brought up in London, of course," she said, as if that was a terrible disadvantage from which few people recovered. I knew she didn't think much of my mother. I'd seen her face when she'd offered me a puppy, and I'd had to tell her my mother was frightened of dogs. I was beginning to get angry, when she said, "I wish you could have known them then, Kate. They were so happy together."

"You mean, before I was born."

She smiled. "Come on, Kate. Don't grudge them a little happiness just because you weren't there." Then she added soberly, "It didn't last long."

Because they'd lost Emma, I thought. But what about me? Why hadn't I made them happy again when I was born?

Miss Wait spent most of the walk back warning me to behave myself. I mustn't throw tantrums. I mustn't upset Rosie, because that would upset my mother. I was bound to be jealous, she said, waving aside my denials— it was only human, but I must learn to swallow it down like medicine, and not make a fuss.

"You can always ring me if you want to scream. I shan't mind. But if I hear you've been misbehaving yourself, I'll skin you."

"I won't," I said.

"On the other hand, if I hear you've been a good girl, I'll give you—let me see—what do you want?"

Rosie to go away, I thought, but did not say it aloud. Instead I told her I'd be good for nothing, to which she replied that she'd always feared so, and we both laughed.

That night I lay in bed waiting for Rosie. She was late. I was beginning to think she'd forgotten or changed her mind, when suddenly she appeared, slipping in quietly and shutting the door behind her.

"You're not asleep then?" she asked.

"No. I was waiting for you."

"Yeh. Well, here I am."

She began to walk inquisitively round my room, staring at everything; the pictures on the wall, my puppets hanging from their hooks, my three dolls on the dressing table, my collection of china animals on the shelves. I noticed that she never once touched anything, but kept her hands clasped behind her back as if afraid she might otherwise be accused of stealing.

"Got a lot of things, ain't you?" she said.

"I suppose so."

"Them china animals. They're ever so pretty. Must be worth a lot."

"You can have one if you like."

She looked at me sharply. "No. Ta all the same. I wasn't hinting. I don't want nothing of yours."

Except my home, I thought, but I did not say it aloud.

There was a long mirror on one wall. She stopped in front of it and began preening herself like a bird, poking her thin fingers into her hair, arranging it into little dark feathers on her forehead. Then she struck a pose, putting her hands on her hips and bunching my second-best nightie into her narrow waist, twisting this way and that to admire the effect.

I lay watching her, as I had often watched my mother when she came up to my room before going out to a party. She used to stand in front of the mirror in just that way, pushing her hair into place, or turning round to admire the long folds of her dress.

It didn't mean anything. Any female in front of a mirror would do the same.

"I thought you wanted to talk about finding your mum," I said.

"Yeh." She left the mirror and came over to sit on the edge of my bed. "I could flipping murder her," she said. "Just wait till I find her. I'll wring her dirty neck."

"I don't blame you. It was beastly of her . . ."

"No, it wasn't!" She turned on me, her voice rising

alarmingly, shrill and loud. "You dunno nothing about
it. She did it for me. Because I said I was fed up with her
and her goings-on. That's why she done it."

"Yes, of course," I agreed hastily, glancing anxiously at the door, expecting my parents to come thun-
dering up the stairs to see what was wrong. Rosie
looked at the door too.

"D'you think they heard?" she whispered.

"I hope not."

She slipped off my bed, crossed to the door, and
opened it. We both held our breath and listened. Then
she shook her head and shut the door again.

"S'all right. Not a peep." She sat down on my bed
and said apologetically, "Sorry I screeched. Forgot. After all, it's not like you knew my mum. Must've seemed
a bit odd. I mean, to anybody who didn't know her."

"What is she like?" I asked.

"Pretty. Ever so pretty. She's got blond hair. Well,
it is now. It was red last year. She's always changing it.
She's very young for a mum. People are always saying
she don't look old enough to . . ." She broke off, biting
her lip.

I thought I knew what she'd been about to say—"to
have a daughter my age." My heart began thudding
uncomfortably.

"You don't think it could be true? I mean, that
you're . . ."

"Your long-lost sister? Don't be daft."

I wanted to ask her why, in that case, her mother
had said she was, but I did not dare. Her face, in the
dim, shaded light, looked very fierce. After a bit she
began talking again, quietly, not looking at me.

"We had a row last week. She'd been at my piggy
bank again, cleaned it out. I wasn't half mad. Thought

she'd put it on a flipping horse and lost the lot. Like she done once before."

"Is she a gambler?" I asked, fascinated.

"No. Well, sometimes. When it rains. You gotta have something to cheer you up. It's all right for you. You dunno what it's like being poor, without no hope of nothing better, not ever. Like Mum says, you gotta give fate a chance to smile on you. But horses are silly—"

"Silly? Why?"

"Oh, if they're any good, the odds ain't. You don't get nothing much even if they win, see? And they don't. Not when Mum backs 'em. They get colic or the going's too wet or too dry or they have spavins. It's a mug's game. I told her so. We didn't half have a slanging match. Could've heard us right down the street. Next day, though, she went all quiet and moody. It was Sunday. She was brought up religious, and Sundays always make her feel bad."

"Bad?"

"Yeh. Suppose it does seem funny. Never thought of that before," Rosie said.

"Do you go to church?" I asked.

"No. Not much. Mum went last Sunday, though, while I got the dinner ready. Didn't seem to cheer her up none. She came back a bit weepy. Kept saying as how she loved me, even if she hadn't been a good mum. Real soppy. D'you know what I been wondering? Perhaps the vicar said something in his sermon about sacrificing yourself for your kids, and that give her the idea to find me a good home."

"You mean, just send you off like that? To someone else's house?"

"You lot get shoved off to boarding schools."

She took my breath away. If she couldn't see the difference, she must be stupid, I thought.

"How did she know about us?" I asked.

"Read it in the Sundays, I suppose. The lady up-stairs lets us have hers when she's done with them. Your dad said there was a bit about your sister being snatched, asked me if we'd seen it. I hadn't. I don't read the papers much. But Mum must have. She was very quiet. I should've guessed she was up to something. . . . I wish I hadn't been so horrid. Turned out she hadn't put my money on a horse after all. She give it to Mrs. Briggs—that's our landlady—to keep her quiet. We owed her a bit and she'd been bothering. I wouldn't have yelled so much if she'd told me that sooner. I said it was all right. I told her. I told her I didn't mind. She didn't have to . . ."

Rosie turned her head away and sniffed. I put my arm round her shoulders and hugged her.

My mind was in a mess. I was terribly tired and my thoughts kept drifting away as they do just before you fall asleep. Confused pictures filled my head . . . a young woman crouched over a piggy bank, sliding the pennies out with the blade of a knife. Her hair was changing from yellow to red, like a traffic light . . . take care . . . stop.

A tune came into my head, but the words were wrong—"she doesn't like Sundays, she doesn't like Sun-days." Now I saw the woman creeping nervously past a row of tall churches, not daring to go in. The sky was like blue writing paper, on which was written "you wont never forgive me i know i done a wicked thing." Now she was kneeling inside a church, her eyes shut, her lips moving silently, "i am sending her back to you better late than never."

Someone was tying me up like a parcel. I jerked awake and saw that it was Rosie, bossily tucking my quilt round me, and giving my pillow officious little slaps, like a child playing nurse.

"Bedtime for you, kiddo," she said, when she saw my eyes were open. "You ain't used to late nights like me, are you? Never mind. We got tomorrow."

She turned off my bedside lamp and made her way to the door in the dark. I saw her silhouette against the light from the landing and heard her say, "Night night. Sleep tight. Take care the fleas don't bite." Then she was gone.

I looked after her, afraid that this thin, sharp stranger might be my sister Emma after all.

No, I thought stubbornly, shutting my eyes. The word NO, printed against the darkness of my closed lids, seemed to grow larger and larger, until there was only room for the O, as smooth and oval as a cuckoo's egg. I knew then that things could never be the same again. Whether Rosie stayed or went away made no difference. My dream of a small, soft, fair-haired sister was pushed out for ever.

11

Nearly a week had passed and Rosie was still here. Nobody would tell me anything. They claimed there was nothing to tell, but I didn't believe them. The house seemed full of whispers and secrets and people talking behind closed doors. Even Mrs. Trapp said, "It's no good asking me, dearie. *I* don't know."

Her fat face looked smug and secretive. She'd been got at. Someone must have said to her, "Don't tell Kate. She'll only make a fuss."

"Why don't you go and play with Rosie," she said, shooing me out of the kitchen.

They all wanted me to play with Rosie. If they saw me by myself, they no longer said "Hullo, Kate," but "Where's Rosie?" accusingly, as if I was her keeper and had fallen down on the job.

Rosie was sitting on the wall in front of our house, swinging her legs and gazing up the road. It was her favorite place. Every day she would sit here watching the people go by on their way to the heath: the dog walkers; children with kites, jam jars, and fishing nets; families with push chairs and picnic baskets. Our road is a dead end. It is shut off from the heath by a row of posts, so there are few cars. I noticed every time one passed, she would lean forward, staring hopefully. Poor Rosie, waiting in vain for her mother to come and take her away.

"Has your mother got a car?" I asked.

"Don't be daft. She ain't even got a bicycle."

I thought about that, then said, "Has she lots of friends?"

"Your dad's already asked me that," she said irritably. "Wanted a list of their names. How'm I supposed to remember their surnames? Never heard 'em—it was all Dick and Harry, Mandy and Bettine. You know, pub friends, or women at the launderette, somebody to have a joke with. She'll have a new crowd now. She won't bother with the old lot."

"Didn't she have a special friend?"

"Boyfriend, d'you mean? Yeah, well, last one was Harry Jenkins, but we ain't seen him for ages. Good riddance. They was talking of getting married, but I wasn't having him for a father, ta very much."

"Didn't you like him?"

"Like him? I hated his guts, the fat hairy ape. He come in drunk once. Couldn't hardly stand up. That cooked his goose. He barged into a table and knocked over Mum's precious vase she'd won at bingo. Cut glass it was—I wish it had cut *him*. When Mum told him off, he swore at her something dreadful."

Rosie repeated what he had said, while I listened, fascinated. I wondered if my parents would be so keen on my playing with her if they knew the tales she told me. My vocabulary was increasing rapidly.

"What happened next?" I asked, and heard my own voice, eager, a little breathless, sounding just as I had imagined Emma's would have done. Everything was upside down.

"Well, Mum wasn't having that," Rosie went on. "She don't like swearing. 'Don't you use bad language to me, you bloody ape,' she said. 'Get out. And don't bother to come back.' He wasn't half mad. I thought he was going for her so I kicked his ankle and started screaming, and the landlady came up and threatened to call the police. He made off so fast, he fell down the steps outside. Laugh! You should've seen him. He'd knocked over one of the trash cans and was lying there, with eggshells and fish heads stuck to him, like a sort of fancy dress. Rubbish Heap, that's what he could have gone as."

Things like that never happened in our family, I thought enviously. My parents never had an open battle. They were more like snipers. Concealed behind the cornflakes packet, they would exchange cold looks or shoot off nasty little remarks they thought I would not understand.

"Mum cried a bit that night," Rosie was saying. "But she promised she'd never marry nobody I couldn't take to. Well, it was only fair. Why should I be lumbered with a dad I didn't like?"

"But supposing she fell in love?" I asked. "Supposing she was swept off her feet?"

I was very romantic then. Often Mrs. Trapp had magazines tucked in her shopping bag, *Real Love* and *Confessions,* things like that. I would slip one out when she wasn't looking, and go and read it in the lavatory. The impression they gave me was that falling in love was like falling off a cliff. There was nothing you could do about it but shut your eyes and hope you'd land soft, with wedding bells ringing in your ears.

"You're silly," Rosie said sharply.

I looked at her. I was getting used to her face. That wooden look—it was like shutters over the windows of a house in which someone was hiding, frightened but ready to shoot it out if attacked.

So I kept quiet. I didn't suggest that her mum might have found someone she wanted to marry. Someone she knew Rosie would not accept. Perhaps he didn't want a ready-made daughter of thirteen and had said, "It's either her or me. You have to choose between us." "A Mother's Choice," I thought, seeing it as a title in a magazine.

Sitting on the wall beside Rosie, with the rough stone warm against my leg and the sun beating down on my head, I tried to form a picture of Rosie's mum. It was like a jigsaw when half the pieces are missing, and you've lost the lid of the box, so that you don't know whether it's going to be a bowl of roses or a field of cows.

The pieces seemed to belong to different puzzles. The guilt-ridden woman who didn't like Sundays, the gambler, the feckless mother who liked to go out to the pub at night or to a dance, and who used to lock Rosie in her room at night when she was small, so that "she wouldn't come to no harm."

"That's awful," I said, sounding prim. "Mummy would never leave me alone."

"So I've noticed," Rosie said sharply. "You want to be careful, kid, or she'll be coming with you on your honeymoon."

"That's not fair. It's only because of Emma. Because of Emma vanishing."

Rosie was silent. She looked away from me and began kicking her heels against the wall. Then she said slowly, "It must've been awful for her. Her baby gone, just like that." She turned to me, her eyes terrified, "Supposing . . . What'll happen if I never find Mum?"

"I don't know," I said. I had wondered that too. Would we have to keep her? Forever? I added quickly, "But you will find her. I know you will. I'll help you."

"I dunno where to look," she said hopelessly.

I had begun to wonder whether my father knew where to look. Every day when he came home, we asked him, "Any news?" and he answered with false cheerfulness, "No, not yet. But don't worry. I'm sure we shall hear something soon."

It must have hurt him to have no success to relate. He hated to be beaten. Even playing Go Fish with me, he always had to win.

I wondered if Rosie was taken in by his optimism. I certainly wasn't. That evening I followed him into his study.

"Not now, Kate," he said when he noticed me. "I've some important telephone calls to make."

"It's always not now," I complained. "You talk to Rosie for ages, but you never have time for me."

"You know perfectly well why I talk to Rosie. I

assure you she doesn't enjoy being asked questions all
the time, poor child. I really think you might try to be a
little more sympathetic." He broke off, and sighed. I
thought how tired he looked. "I'm sorry, Kate," he said.
"What did you want?"

"Do you really think you'll find Rosie's mum?"

"Of course. It's merely a matter of time."

(The brush-off. Don't tell Kate we're worried.
Don't tell her anything. Did he think I was stupid?)

"But supposing you don't?" I asked.

His eyes were already straying to some papers on
his desk. "We will," he said firmly. "Everything possible's being done. I've put the matter into the hands of
a firm of detectives."

"The same ones who couldn't find Emma?" I
asked.

It was the wrong thing to say, of course. I swear I
had not meant it nastily. It just slipped out. There was
no reason for him to be so cross with me.

Rosie was in a bad mood too. Restless. Snappy. She
didn't want to play in the garden. She didn't want to
watch television.

"I think I'll go out for a bit," she announced after
supper.

There was a pause. Then my mother said brightly,
"What a good idea, Rosie. It's a beautiful evening. Let's
all go."

Rosie drew in her breath with a hiss. My mother's
smile wavered and she added pleadingly, "Won't that
be nice?"

Silence. Then Rosie let her breath out again,
slowly, harmlessly.

"Yeh. Ever so," she said without expression.

Later, sitting on the end of my bed, she told me she was sorry for my mother.

"But it ain't no good. I can't turn into her baby just to keep her happy, can I? I mean, it's like a flipping prison here. I dunno how you stand it." She got up restlessly and went to look out of the window, "Nothing to see but stupid trees. . . . I got to get out. I got to do something. I dunno. Go back home and ask around a bit. Mum might've said something."

"But you've already done that," I said, for my father had driven her over to Hockley twice last week.

"Yeh. But with your dad there . . . I mean, he's sort of official-looking. They mightn't like to say. They wouldn't want to get Mum into no trouble. It'd be different with just me."

"Can I come?"

She looked at me without enthusiasm. "Would your mum let you out by yourself?"

"I wouldn't be by myself. I'd be with you."

"Why do you want to come?"

I was simply curious to see where she had lived, but I did not think this was a wise reason to give, so I said, "I want to help you, Rosie."

She muttered something under her breath that I did not hear. I had a feeling it was not complimentary. It was plain she did not want me.

"Please, Rosie."

"Would your mum let us go by ourselves?" she asked.

I hesitated, remembering that Mrs. Trapp had said Hockley was a rough part of London.

"I think it would be better if we pretended we were going somewhere else. Not so far, I mean, just so she wouldn't worry." I thought for a moment, and then said, "We could say we wanted to go to the zoo."

I couldn't think why Rosie laughed. "Oh, ta very much," she said. "Don't mind my feelings, will you?"

12

I wished I did not feel so guilty. My mother had not wanted to let us go out on our own, but my father had said impatiently, "Good heavens, Margaret, they'll be perfectly all right. They're both sensible girls. What on earth do you imagine can happen to them at the zoo?"

I wished we were safe at the zoo, among the lions and tigers and snakes. I didn't like the look of Hockley. I didn't like the stink of it or the way it roared. It was like a huge concrete cave, a place for monsters to breed in.

We'd come out of the underground station into a wide and dreary street. The gray-faced, anonymous buildings, once offices or factories perhaps, were derelict; their windows boarded up, their walls stained and scribbled on. Large letters in white paint caught my eye: GO HOME. I felt it was addressed to me.

There were no people on the pavements. Everything was on the road, racing past us, anxious to be gone. Huge juggernauts, vans, buses, cars, and motorbikes roared by, shaking the dust from their wheels. The metal clamor in the dead streets made me nervous.

Rosie was saying something. I couldn't hear her.
"What?"

"Come on," she mouthed, and taking hold of my elbow, hurried me along the pavement and into a slit of an alley between tall buildings—a dirty, rancid alley, so narrow that the sun missed it altogether. It was full of shadows and dark doorways. Wet stains discolored the filthy paving. Tattered garbage bags, like black blisters, oozed a foul pus of decay.

I was frightened. Every shadow seemed to move towards me. I would be murdered . . . serve me right for venturing out from behind our high walls . . . why had Rosie brought me here?

I looked at her sharply, and as if feeling my glance, she turned and smiled at me. An open smile, friendly and innocent. She began to whistle cheerfully. I wished I were young enough to hold her hand.

She was walking confidently, dodging the rubbish with an almost dancing step. In the train she had made up her face, crouching over a small mirror, her little finger resting on her chin to steady her hand. Now her eyes were bright beneath blue lids and her whistling lips glistened pale as an ice crystal against her brown skin.

How different she looked. She looked happy.

Our house in its leafy street, the wholesome meals, the comfortable bed, had all left her cold. She wanted the world she knew. She wanted to go home.

Home? She didn't have a home anymore. . . .

"Where are we going?" I asked, but she only said, "Hurry up."

We came out of the dark alley into a blaze of color. We were in a market. Stalls lined the street on either side. Fruit and vegetables, old clothes and new china. Handbags and leather belts. Pink nylon, flowered cotton, silver bracelets from India, glass beads from Birmingham.

"Watch out!" a man said as I slipped on a squashed cabbage leaf and bumped against his stall. Then he caught sight of Rosie. "Hullo, sweetheart. Haven't seen you around lately. Bin on your holidays?"

"No. You ain't seen my mum, have you?" she asked.

"Your mum? Can't say I 'ave. Not today."

"What about yesterday? Or the day before?"

His small eyes were suddenly sharp. " 'Ow long she bin gone, Rosie love?" he asked, not unkindly. "She ain't left you on yer own, 'as she?"

"No. It's all right," Rosie said, wriggling her shoulders. "I just wondered if you'd seen her about, that's all."

He looked at her, rubbing his thumb over his chin thoughtfully. Then he shouted, "Hey, Elsie, 'ave you seen Louise Martin around lately?"

The woman at the next stall (towels and sheets), turned round. I don't think she noticed us. Her round face assumed an expression of enjoyable gloom. " 'Aven't you 'eard?" she asked, seeming unable to believe her luck. "She's gone off. Left 'er little girl locked in 'er room. Tied to a bedpost. Starving she was when they found 'er, poor little mite."

The man, embarrassed, tried to stop her but it was no good. She was in full spate. "Bones. Nothing but bones and bruises," she said. "The doctors don't think she'll live. 'Anging's too good for that woman, if you ask me."

Rosie, who had been standing listening with her mouth open, recovered her breath.

"Dying, am I?" she screamed at the top of her voice. "Starving, am I?" Heads turned. A small crowd began to gather. "You fat liar, I'll have you! Bruises, is it?" She turned to the crowd, pulling her sleeves back to show her shoulders. "Look at me. D'you see any bruises? Look at my legs." She pulled up her short skirt, revealing her pink panties. A youth at the back whistled.

"Now, Rosie," the kind man said awkwardly, but she ignored him.

"Not a mark on me, is there?" she demanded. "Mum never laid a finger on me in my life. I'll have you. Spreading lies—that's libel. Ain't it?" she said, turning to me. "Her dad's a lawyer," she announced proudly. "She knows all about it."

All eyes were on me. I wished I could hide. My cheeks were burning.

"It's slander," I said. My voice sounded thin and precise. They looked at me with interest, as if I were a talking dog, and waited for some further pronouncement. I searched my memory. "Defamation of character," I added.

Rosie seized on the phrase gleefully. "Deformation of character," she said, rolling the words on her tongue. "D'you hear that? She's been deforming my mum. Before witnesses. You can go to prison for that. You tell 'em, Kate. She can go to prison for that, can't she?"

I wished I could hide under a stall. They were all looking at me again, waiting for me to speak as respectfully as if I were a High Court judge.

"I think so," I said uncertainly.

"I was only saying wot I 'eard, miss," the fat woman said to me. Her face was red and frightened. "I didn't mean no 'arm. It's only wot everybody says." She appealed to the bystanders. "They've no right to pick on me. Everybody knows Louise Martin's a bad lot."

"You hear that?" Rosie screamed. "You hear that, all of you? Deformation. Ten years you'll get for that, you old bag."

"Now, Rosie," the kind man said again. "Leave off, there's a good girl."

But someone at the back of the crowd shouted encouragingly, "Go it, Rosie! Let 'er 'ave it!"

Rosie needed no encouragement. "You're going to get it. You're going to get it!" she jeered, jumping up and down in front of the fat woman, who lost her temper and yelled back, "It's your no-good mum 'oo's gonna get it. There bin questions asked. May, you tell 'er about that man wot come round asking questions . . ."

A thin woman in a blue dress looked embarrassed and began edging back, mumbling, "I don't know, I'm sure."

"Oo, you liar!" the fat woman squealed indignantly. She appealed to the crowd. "It was 'er wot told me. You ask 'er. Ask 'er about that man wot came round. . . . You come back 'ere, May Watson!"

But the thin woman had slipped away and was hurrying down the street, with Rosie running after her and the crowd cheering her on.

I tried to follow them, but the fat woman caught hold of my arm.

"You don't want to 'ave nothing to do with them, dear. That Mrs. Martin's no better than she should be. You don't want to believe a word they say. 'Mrs. Martin' she calls 'erself, but I know better."

I hated the look in her eyes and the smell of her breath, and I pulled away from her.

"Don't say I didn't warn you," she shrieked after me. "Nothing but trouble."

I could not see Rosie. The people gave way for me willingly enough. One of them said kindly, "That's it. You stick up for your friend. Rosie's all right. She's a good girl."

There was no sign of her. I was through the crowd now, running down between the stalls with the people looking after me. A man stepped out and barred my way.

"Hey, what's your hurry?" he asked suspiciously. "What's been going on?"

"I want Rosie," I said, nearly crying. "I've lost Rosie."

"Rosie Martin? She went that way." He pointed up a side road. "Cheer up, love. You'll soon find her."

I ran the way he pointed. It was a short street. Empty except for an old woman sweeping the pavement in front of a café. She didn't even look up as I ran past her.

Now I was in a shopping street, crowded with strangers. Everywhere I looked there were people— thin, fat, short, tall—but none of them Rosie. Rosie had vanished.

I stood there helplessly as they jostled past me. I couldn't see over their heads. I didn't know which way to go. I was lost . . . and I had lost Rosie.

There was no going home. I couldn't go home without her. My father would be furious and shout at me. "How could you?" he'd say. "Look what happens when we trust you." My mother would be worried sick. She would have a migraine, and lie in a dark room, with an iron band tightening round her head and sharp lights pecking at her eyes. . . . Rosie had vanished, just like Emma, and it was all my fault. They would never forgive me.

I burst into tears.

13

I was used to people paying attention to me when I cried. Comforting me. Asking me what the matter was. Offering me handkerchiefs.

Now I stood weeping on the pavement and nobody took any notice. They walked past me, intent on their own concerns. Occasionally, through the watery blur of my tears, I saw a face turning to look at me, but no one stopped. I was nothing to them. Just one more crying child in the world. I had never felt so horribly unimportant before.

I don't know how long I stood there before someone noticed me: it was an attention I could have done without.

> "Cry, baby, cry,
> Put your finger in your eye . . ."

Two small boys were jeering at me.

"Go away," I said thickly. "Leave me alone."

"Go away," one of them mimicked. "Leave me alone."

"Yer nose is running," the other said. "Catch it if yer can."

I turned on them, raising my fist, and they ran off giggling.

Pulling my hanky out of my pocket, I wiped my face as best I could, and tried to think what to do. I had money. I could go home. Why should I worry about Rosie? She could look after herself. This was where she belonged, not with us. . . . But it was no good. I knew I would have to find her. I just couldn't go home alone.

I began walking back towards the market. That's where she would expect me to be waiting, if she thought of me at all. That's where she'd come back to, if coming back had ever been her intention.

Rosie was sitting on an upturned crate beside an antique stall. Her back was towards me.

"I dunno," she was saying to the woman behind the stall. "I just went off for a second and when I come back, she'd flipping gone. Her dad'll skin me if I go back without her. I got to find her."

She did not seem to be trying to find me very hard. She sat there quite at her ease in the sun, eating an apple, her legs stretched out in front of her. .

"She'll be all right, darling," the woman said, in a clear voice that carried conviction a long way, right to the back of the stalls—even the market stalls. She was a small, dark woman, with pretty hands that moved as she talked, as if blown about by her breath. "Take my advice and stay put. It's a great mistake to go chasing after people. You just go round in circles"—her hands drew invisible worlds in the air—"and keep missing each other. I believe in letting people find me. Much the best thing. She's bound to come back to the market, isn't she?"

"Dunno," Rosie said. "There's no telling what she'll do. She's such a baby. Never been out by herself before, would you believe it? Eleven years old and never been out without her mummy."

I felt my cheeks flushing angrily. At that moment I hated Rosie. I drew back behind a rack of secondhand clothes. I did not want her to see me with my face still blotched and swollen from crying.

"Now, that's a mistake," the woman said. "It doesn't do to mollycoddle children. You don't want them to grow up soft. It's a hard world, take it from me, darling. I know. Granite."

"Oh, she ain't so bad really," Rosie said. "Bit wet, but I seen worse."

I could have hit her. Who did she think she was?

I had not meant to eavesdrop, honestly. I'd only wanted to give the tearstains time to fade from my cheeks before facing Rosie. But now nothing would have moved me away from my hiding place. At least, unless . . . I glanced uneasily over my shoulder. The owner of the old clothes was sitting at the other end of his stall, reading a newspaper, and had not noticed me. Which was just as well, as the rack held only men's clothes, ancient overcoats smelling of dust and dry-cleaning fluid. A sneeze was my greatest danger. I looked back.

"Heard anything from your mum yet, Rosie?" the woman was saying.

"No."

"Don't worry. I'm sure she's all right."

Rosie did not answer, but flipped her apple core across the street as if she hoped it would hit someone.

"I suppose . . ." the woman began. She picked up a silver chain from her stall and started playing with it. "I suppose—now don't panic, darling, I'm not suggesting the worst—but have you tried the hospitals?"

"We done that last week," Rosie said. "Mr. Seton got his clerk to call around. They didn't find nothing."

"Oh, darling," the woman said, clasping her hands together and pressing them against her yellow silk blouse. "Darling, what a relief."

I hoped she would ask who Mr. Seton was. I wanted to hear what Rosie would say about us. But just then a customer came up to the stall and they were silent. He glanced at everything briefly, then picked up an oval dish decorated with flowers and birds, and examined it closely. Turned it over and peered at the back. Held it over his head like a sunshade and squinted up at it.

"I could let you have it for fifty pounds," the woman said.

"Fifty pounds!" he said, sounding as shocked as I was. "You must be joking."

"It's Royal Worcester. Eighteenth century."

"Is that what you bought it as? You've been done, love. It's a fake." He put it back on its stand. "Hold it up to the light," he advised, and walked away.

"Pig," the woman said. She lifted up the dish and stared at it. Shrugged as if she did not know what she was supposed to be looking for. "I'm always being had," she said. "I don't know why I do this. My agent advised me to. He would. He hasn't got me a part for months." She put the dish down again and frowned at it. "Wretched thing."

"It's ever so pretty," Rosie said.

"Not much good, darling, if it's not genuine. It's got to be the real thing."

"The real thing," Rosie repeated slowly. Then she said, "D'you think I'm like my mum, Mrs. Blake?"

"Like her?" The woman sounded surprised. "Well, no, not really, are you? I expect you take after your father. Girls often do."

"Did you know my dad?"

"No, darling."

"Mum said he had ginger hair and a mustache."

"Well," the woman said after a pause, "perhaps you take after a granny."

"Perhaps I do, perhaps I don't," Rosie said. "Perhaps I ain't really me at all."

I held my breath. Rosie, who had seemed so sure who she was—was she beginning to have doubts now?

"Darling, I know exactly how you feel," the woman was saying. "Sometimes when I look into a mirror in the morning, I think, 'No, really, I can't bear it. This isn't me at all.'"

I wished I could see Rosie's face, but she still had her back to me. I wondered what she was thinking.

Then she said, "D'you think the name Rosie suits me?"

"It's a pretty name."

"Yeh, but d'you think it suits me? Do I look like a Rosie?"

"Well, I don't know, darling. You could do with a bit more color."

"What about Emma? Do I look like an Emma?"

No, I wanted to say. No.

The woman laughed. "What's in a name?" she asked, in such ringing tones that heads turned. "Shakespeare, darling. The balcony scene from *Romeo and Juliet*. I played Juliet my first year in rep. Down in Brighton." She put both hands on the edge on her stall and leaned over it as if it were a balcony.

"What's in a name? that which we call a rose
By any other name would smell as sweet."

"If you ask me, he didn't know what he was talking about," Rosie muttered. "This Rose would smell a lot sweeter in some people's noses if her name was Emma."

The woman looked at her with sudden concern.

"What is it, Rosie? What's all this about Emma? Is that the little girl—I thought you said she was called Kate. Is she being horrid to you?"

"No. It's just . . . oh, I dunno." Rosie got up and stood by the stall, picking things up and putting them down again. "They got me muddled. There was this woman looked me over like I was a horse. My chin was wrong. My eyes was right. Only I mustn't smile, see? Or they was wrong again. I tell you, they're all nutters there. I'll end up like them if I ain't careful."

She picked up a hand mirror from the stall. Peering over the clothes rack, I could just see the dim blur of her face reflected in the glass.

"Same old face," she said. "Ain't changed none. Same eyes, same nose, same mouth. Just lost my label. Dunno why it should matter, but . . . D'you know what he told me?"

"Who, darling?"

"That Mr. Seton. He said there wasn't no trace of me at Somerset House—that's where they keep all the records of births and deaths and things."

"Yes, I know, darling."

"They said I hadn't been born. Hadn't lived. Hadn't died. No Rosie Martin anywhere 'oo could be me. That was a nice thing to say, wasn't it? Lost my mum. Lost my name. Lost myself. Just a walking nobody, that's me."

I saw her back stiffen suddenly. Too late I realized what she had seen in the mirror—another face behind her own, a round-eyed face peeping over a coatrack. Me.

14

"Look 'oo's here," Rosie said as I emerged sheepishly from behind the clothes rack. "How long you been hiding in gents' overcoats?"

"Like a little moth, darling," the woman said, and laughed.

"Miss Eyes-and-Ears, that's her. Always watching and listening and creeping about."

But Rosie was too pleased to have found me again to be really cross. She said good-bye to the woman, and taking me firmly by the hand, led me into a narrow street.

"Where are we going?"

"To the Green Man."

"Who?"

"It's a pub. Where Mum used to meet her friends. Come on."

Our progress was slow. Too many people knew Rosie. Too many people had heard the gossip about her.

"How are you, dear?" they'd ask, fencing us in with their shopping baskets. "Better now? We 'eard you was in 'ospital."

And Rosie would start screeching at them, while I blushed and tried to drag her away. Once she was surrounded by a crowd of her friends, who greeted her with shrill cries of welcome.

"Hullo, stranger. Where you been?"

"Why wasn't you at the disco Saturday?"

"Thought you was in hospital."

I stood patiently on the hot pavement, unnoticed and ignored. I could not blame Rosie for not introducing me to her friends. After all, I hadn't let her meet mine, but had made excuses not to see them whenever they had rung me, knowing my mother would make me take Rosie too. Once, putting down the telephone after an elaborate lie, I'd turned to see Rosie behind me, looking at me with a smile as thin and bitter as lemon peel, as if she'd guessed why I was doing it.

She thought I was a snob. She was right. I was. I disliked myself for it, but I just couldn't help it.

"Kate? Kate?" She was calling me now. "Where's that flipping kid gone? Can't turn your back on her a minute. . . . Kate? Where are you?"

Her friends took it up. "Kate, Kate, where are you, Kate?" they shrieked, until the whole street rang with my name.

"I'm here," I said, stepping out of the doorway in which I'd been standing. They laughed, pushed me towards Rosie, and went rollicking down the street. All except one, a tall, dark youth, who looked at me with disfavor.

"She's too little," he said.

"Yeh," Rosie agreed.

"She'll 'ave to stay outside."

"Yeh."

"I can get you in but not her."

"No."

I suppose I was stupid at first but I could not think what they meant. Then Rosie explained that children under fourteen were not allowed in pubs.

"Don't you know nothing?" she asked impatiently.

"You're not fourteen," I pointed out resentfully, and the youth spread his hands out, as if asking the world to witness what a fool I was.

"That's right. Tell everybody. Write a letter to the landlord, why don't you?"

The Green Man was on the next corner. It was a
dismal building, decorated with cracked green tiles the
color of pond water. A large sign on the wall said TAKE
COURAGE. Good advice, I thought as Rosie and the
youth vanished through the door. Without a word to
me. Without telling me how long they would be, or
offering to bring me out some lemonade.

I stood on the pavement, hot, cross, and thirsty,
and scowled. The door was propped open, but three
men were standing just inside, blocking my view. I
watched them for a moment; then, when they showed
no signs of moving, I began to walk round the pub,
trying to see through the windows.

It wasn't easy. The glass was obscured, partly by an
elaborate engraving of flowers and leaves and partly by
a thin coating of dust. I could see people dimly through
the frosted garlands, like ghosts in a garden. I rubbed a
patch clear of dirt with my hanky and looked again.

Rosie was sitting talking to a middle-aged woman,
both so close to me that, but for the glass, I could almost
have touched them. I could see their mouths opening
and shutting, but I could not hear a word. It was like
watching my goldfish in their tank.

Rosie's face was tight with excitement. Whatever
the woman was saying was plainly important. Then
Rosie must have asked a question, for the woman
looked at her watch and nodded, waving her arm as if
to say "Yes, there's time if you go now." I saw Rosie get
up and ducked out of sight.

When she came hurrying out of the pub, I was
standing exactly where she had left me, looking innocent. I don't think she was pleased to see me. She hesitated for a moment, as if wondering what to do with
me. I felt if there had been a mailbox nearby, she'd
have mailed me home. But she shrugged and said,

THE CUCKOO SISTER   97

"Come on, kid. Quick," and began running down the street.

Her legs were longer than mine. I ran after her, full of questions I had no breath to put, seeing with dismay the distance widen between us. She disappeared round a corner and I was sure I would lose her again. But when I reached it, I saw to my relief that she had stopped halfway down the next street and was looking back.

As I ran up, she came to meet me and said, "Go into this café and wait for me. I just got to see someone."

"Who?"

"Nobody you know. A woman—one of Mum's friends."

"Can't I come?"

"No, you can't. It ain't nothing to do with you." She was almost dancing with impatience. "Oh, go and . . . have a milkshake or something. Leave me alone, can't you!"

I turned and went into the café without another word. I sat down at one of the tables and picked up the menu. Began counting under my breath. When I had reached ten, I put the menu down and went out again, leaving the waitress to stare.

I was just in time to see Rosie go into a shop on the other side of the road. MARY'S MERRY-GO-WASH it said in chrome letters above a glass shopfront. It was a launderette. Even from here I could see the double row of white machines and the orange plastic chairs, on which a few people sat, staring at the soapy portholes like bored passengers on a dull cruise.

There was too much glass. Nowhere for a watcher to conceal herself. I hesitated, and then crossed the road obliquely, and keeping close to the shop next to the launderette, sidled towards it like a crab. At last, flattening myself against a pillar, I poked my head round and stared through the glass.

Rosie was clasped in the arms of a plump woman with short, bleached hair.

Her mum, I thought. She's found her mum.

Funny. I should have been overjoyed, but I wasn't. One of the washing machines began to shudder, coming to the end of its cycle, with everything whirling round and round, pressed tight to the drum and a dark hole in the middle. That's just how I felt. Whirling and empty.

Then the woman released Rosie and stood back, smiling at her. There was a name embroidered on her pink nylon overall: Bettine.

Bettine? Not Louise?

It was like when you toss a coin to decide between two things. When it comes down heads, you're disappointed. It must have been tails you wanted all the time. So you toss again and this time it comes down tails. And still you're disappointed. I didn't want Rosie to go. I didn't want her to stay. I wanted another choice, a third side to the coin.

They were talking together now, the woman smiling at Rosie, but rather anxiously, I thought. She must have been the manager. There was a table beside her, with a teapot on it, and a mug still steaming; a cashbox, a big packet of soap powder, and little towers of plastic containers. She took one of these, glanced inside it to see if it was clean, and then picked up the teapot.

Rosie shook her head and held out her hand, as if she wanted something different.

The woman hesitated; then she opened her handbag and took out an envelope. From this she extracted a letter, which she gave to Rosie.

Rosie was shaking. The bright blue writing paper

fluttered in her hand, just as the other letter had fluttered in my mother's hand that day in the garden. She sat down on a chair abruptly and began to read. The woman watched her. Then she turned and filled the plastic cup from the pot, put in three spoonfuls of sugar, stirred it carefully, and put it down on the table by Rosie.

We had done first aid at school. Hot sweet tea. Treatment for shock. I knew before I saw Rosie crumple the letter furiously in her hand that there was no happiness for her in those bright blue pages.

The woman, Bettine, comforted her. Patted her shoulder, stroked her hair, and then sat on the edge of the table and began talking earnestly. I could not hear what she said, but she seemed to be explaining, soothing—perhaps making excuses for the writer of the letter. For Rosie's mum.

Rosie sat as if she'd turned to stone, holding the crushed paper tightly in one fist.

The woman urged her to drink the tea, holding out the cup, but Rosie shook her head. She began smoothing out the crumpled letter on the table, ironing it with her fingers. Then she looked up and said something. I think it must have been "Can I keep it?", because when the woman nodded, she folded it over and over into a small square and put it carefully into the side pocket of her skirt.

She got up. The woman fussed round her, putting her hand on Rosie's arm, trying to persuade her to stay, following her between the lines of whirling, roaring machines to the door.

I dodged back out of sight, and heard the woman say, "Don't go, Rosie. I'll be off in half an hour. We can have dinner together. Don't rush off like this."

"I'm all right."

"But Rosie, dear . . ."
"Leave me alone!"
I pressed back against the pillar. Rosie walked past me, staring straight in front of her. Not noticing me. Not remembering me. Walking quickly away to nowhere.

"Rosie! Rosie, wait for me!" I shouted.

She turned round slowly and stared at me. It was such a peculiar look. I don't know how to describe it. Sort of questioning. Uncertain. Curious. As if she was seeing me for the very first time.

15

I longed to know what was in the letter, but it was obvious that Rosie did not want to talk. Her lips were pressed tightly together, and she walked through the summer streets as if locked in a private winter.

Slipping my hand into hers, so that she would have something warm to hold on to, I walked beside her in silence. We were both thinking about the letter. The only difference was that she knew what was in it and I did not.

I don't think she noticed where she was going. We passed the café. The smell of fish and chips and vinegar made my mouth water. I was hungry. It seemed wrong to think of food when Rosie was so unhappy, but I couldn't help it.

"Rosie, how about lunch?"

She did not answer. I don't think she heard me. We walked on and on, and must have gone round in a circle, for suddenly there was the Green Man again, on the next corner. As we approached it, three youths came tumbling out, laughing and jostling each other. One of them was the tall, dark boy who had taken Rosie into the pub. Catching sight of her, he left his friends and came over.

"Did yer 'ave any luck?" he asked.

Rosie shook her head and tried to push past him. He put his arm round her shoulder and said, "Come on, Rosie, let's 'ave it. You c'n tell me. I'm on yer side. Yer mum gone off with someone, 'as she?"

"I hate her!" Rosie said, and burst into tears.

The youth's name was Tony. He went to the same school as Rosie, and was the older brother of one of her friends. There were things about him I did not like, mainly his habit of referring to me as "the kid" and asking Rosie in an audible aside how she'd got lumbered with me, and couldn't she dump me someplace. But he was very kind to Rosie.

She cried noisily, gulping and snorting into his shoulder. Though he rolled his eyes at his friends in comic embarrassment, he held her tightly, patting her shoulder and saying, "That's right, sweet'eart. Don't mind me T-shirt. It c'n do with a wash."

When Rosie had calmed down, he asked her if she had had anything to eat, and finding she had not, took us off to a café and ordered hamburgers and chips and peas for three. I began to like him better then, but I don't think his feelings for me improved any.

On the way there, he and Rosie had walked in front, leaving me to trail behind. The street was crowded and noisy, and I was frightened of getting lost again. I kept so close to their heels that once or twice I trod on them, and was shouted at for not looking where I was going. Accused of eavesdropping. It wasn't true. Their heads were too close together. No one could have heard what they were saying. Only occasionally, bub-

bles of anger from Rosie would rise above the noise of
the traffic: "Pig! Pig! Pig!" . . . "I'll skin her!" . . .
"Broke her promise."

When we reached the café, Rosie muttered something about looking a fright, and went off to the Ladies
to wash her smudged face. Tony began cleaning his
nails with a penknife, ignoring me.

Curiosity gave me courage. Thinking he would
snub me if I asked a direct question, I tried to pretend I
knew all about it.

"It's a shame about Rosie's mum, isn't it?" I said.

He shrugged. "Depends 'ow you look at it, don't it?
Me dad would say she'd left it a bit late in the day, I
mean, what with Rosie and all. But then 'e's old-fashioned."

I nodded, pretending I knew what he was talking
about. I didn't. It made it a bit difficult to know what to
say next. Fortunately, after a pause in which he tapped
the table impatiently and looked round for the waitress,
he went on, "Know what I think? It could turn out for
the best. Rosie'll get over it. And if you ask me, they'll
'ave a better 'ome now than they ever 'ad. A proper
'ome. Mind, it was a bit mean, 'er mum slipping off
without a word. Dunno that I blame 'er, though. 'Ave
you 'eard Rosie when she lets rip?"

I nodded, and we smiled at each other.

"She can't 'alf shriek, our Rosie," he said, almost
admiringly. "Like a blooming knife through yer 'ead,
ain't it? She'd 'ave let 'em 'ave it in both lugs. She
always 'ated 'er mum 'aving men friends. Wanted to
keep 'er to 'erself, Gawd knows why. Louise wasn't my
idea of a mum, know what I mean?"

"What was she like?"

"Louise? Oh, I dunno. Acted a bit like a kid 'erself.
Me mum couldn't never stand 'er. Said she was the sort

of woman who'd save a kitten from drowning and then forget to feed it. More of a leaking tap than a bleeding 'eart, know what I mean? It wasn't fair on Rosie, 'er 'aving to manage everything. I mean, she's only a kid 'erself. Me mum got quite worked up about it at times. Said as 'ow . . . Still, now she's got a 'usband, 'e'll 'ave to cope. Poor beggar."

I stared at him with my mouth open. Two and two came together in my mind with a crash like thunder. I saw it all now.

Rosie's mum had got married. She'd sneaked off behind Rosie's back, without asking her approval, without even telling her. And now she and her new husband were on their honeymoon. I wondered which of them had had the bright idea of parking Rosie on us, pretending she was Emma.

It was all over now. She was not my lost sister after all. She had been Rosie Martin all the time. Rosie Something-else now. She had a stepfather.

I watched her as she came out of the Ladies. Her face was still slightly smudged, but she had put on fresh lipstick and combed her hair. I think she was ashamed of having cried. Her dark eyes looked out defiantly from beneath her spiky fringe.

It's no good trying to look like the boy in the photograph now, I thought. You're not a Seton. You're nothing to do with us. When your mum comes back from her honeymoon, they'll come and take you away. No, they would hardly dare face my father. They'd write her a letter on bright blue writing paper, hidden in a white envelope. And then Rosie would slip away in the night, and we would never see her again. She would vanish, as Emma had done.

I wondered why I did not feel happier about it. Perhaps I was sorry for her. I wondered if my mother would cry when she had gone, feeling she had lost Emma all over again.

We went to the zoo after all. When we left the café, the youth went off, kissing Rosie's cheek and telling her to cheer up, and even waving good-bye to me. I think he was glad to get away. I saw him go bounding down the street like a dog let off the lead.

Rosie had seemed almost cheerful during the meal. She and Tony had talked, not about her mum, but about people they both knew and I did not. I had not minded being left out. I was planning what I would say to Rosie when we were left alone. I had the first words mapped out: "Rosie, I'm sorry about your mum," I would say. "Tony told me about it." She would confide in me then, crying a little, and I would comfort her, telling her it wasn't so-bad having a father. I'd say the sort of things people were always saying to me—"You don't want to make your mother unhappy, do you?" And she'd shake her head and smile. We would go off together to choose them a wedding present, the best of friends, now we did not have to be sisters.

It was a nice scene, the one I had imagined. Pity it did not work out like that.

I began all right. "Rosie, I'm sorry . . ." I said, but before I could get any further, she swore at me, telling me when she wanted my puking sympathy, she'd ask for it. She looked so fierce, I thought she was going to hit me. Her grief seemed to have changed into a wild hatred. She hated everyone she saw—the women passing by in their summer dresses, the whistling boy on his bicycle, the child pushing a doll's pram down the pavement—and me. Especially me.

I didn't know what to do. I was too young. My chin began to tremble. I cry very easily, like my mother,

though I try hard not to. Putting my hand up to my
mouth, I bit my finger, which sometimes works. It
didn't now. I could feel the tears leaking out of my eyes,
and turned my head away.

But she had noticed.

"Don't you start. What've you got to cry about?"
she said. The wildness had died out of her voice. She
sounded like an older sister, impatient but not unkind.
"Blow your nose, that's right. You do look a mess. Got a
comb? Oh, well, have to use mine. It's okay, I ain't got
nits." She began combing my hair, teasing out the tan-
gles gently enough, although at first she seemed to forget I had ears and nearly removed one. "There, that's
better," she said when she had finished. As she in-
spected me, the odd, questioning look came again, as if
she was trying to find the answer to some riddle in my
face, but the writing was too faint to be read.

Then she turned away and said, "Might as well go
to the zoo. We got time. Let's go and see the other
apes."

So I never got my piece said, and there were no
confidences between us. We took the train to Regent's
Park. The sun had gone in but the day was still hot. The
sky was a sort of dirty yellow. I usually liked the zoo,
but, I don't know why, it depressed me that afternoon.
The animals looked as if they resented being stared at.

When we got home, the house was crowded with
my relations; my grandmother, one of my uncles, two
aunts and Miss Wait. As we came into the sitting room,
all heads turned. They too had come to stare. Not at me
but at Rosie.

She looked back at them. Then she ran out of the
room, slamming the door behind her. We could hear
her footsteps running up the stairs and then the sound
of another door slamming in the distance.

"What's the matter? Has anything happened?" my mother asked.

Before I could answer, my father said accusingly, "Kate, what have you done? Have you quarreled with Rosie?"

I hated him. I wasn't going to tell him anything now. Let him find out for himself.

16

"There are too many of us. We've frightened the poor child away," my grandmother said. "We shouldn't have all come together. It was a silly idea of yours, Elizabeth."

"Nonsense," Miss Wait said cheerfully. "Much nicer for her to get us over quickly. Like the dentist. And you did say you wanted to see the girl."

"I could have come down on my own. I'm not too old to travel by myself," my grandmother said tartly. "There was no need for the rest of you to come."

My mother murmured something polite (and untrue) about being delighted to see them all, and made for the door.

"I'll just go up and see Rosie," she said, and slipped out.

I followed her into the hall. Although I was quiet, she heard me and turned round.

"No, Kate. I think it's better if I go alone. Please, darling."

In the shadowy light, her fair, faded hair looked gray. Her skin was dry and lined. She seemed somehow brittle, like a discarded chrysalis from which the butterfly has long flown.

She's grown old, I thought. She's old and I never even noticed.

"Have you got a headache, Mummy?" I asked. She often has a headache when my father's family visit us. Their voices are all so loud.

"No, darling. At least, only a little one. Do go back into the sitting room, Kate. You haven't seen your aunts and uncle for some time. They'll want to talk to you."

"No, they won't. They want to talk about Rosie," I said, but she was already halfway up the stairs. I waited, expecting to hear Rosie shout at her to go away. I heard the door open and close, and then there was silence.

What were they doing? Was Rosie crying and my mother comforting her, stroking her hair as she used to stroke mine when I was upset? Was Rosie confiding in her, telling her things she had not told me, showing her the letter? Was I being shut out again?

I stood alone in the hall, with my hands clenched and a dull pain in my heart.

The sitting room door was open and I could hear them talking inside. About Rosie, of course, not about me. They had forgotten me.

"Well, I think you're foolish not to let the police know," Aunt Isobel was saying. "They could hardly do a worse job than your detectives. The sooner you find that woman, the better. It's an impossible situation for that poor child."

(She meant Rosie. It did not occur to them that it might be difficult for me too.)

"I hardly think it would improve matters if I set the police after her precious mum," my father said. "Rosie would never forgive me. I've given her my promise I will do no such thing."

"That's all very well, but you don't want to put yourself in a false position. After all, that woman has committed a crime, whichever way you look at it. Either baby snatching in the past or attempted fraud now. You be careful you don't find yourself arrested as an accessory or something."

"Come off it, Isobel," Miss Wait said. "What do you know about it? Anthony's the solicitor, not you. He should know."

"Oh, yes, I'm the solicitor," my father said. "If this had happened to one of my clients, I'd have advised him to notify the proper authorities, to have a blood test done on the child at once, and preferably arrange for her to be cared for by a third party until the case was decided. Then I'd have sat back in my chair and wondered why he'd done none of these things. Well, I know now. When you're faced with a bewildered and unhappy child, you don't give a damn for the proper procedures. Rosie is the most important consideration here, and everything else must come second."

(Move over, Kate, I thought. Make way for Rosie. You've got to take second place now.)

I wanted to shout at them that Rosie had only been sent to us because her mother wanted to get married and was afraid she would make a fuss. You don't have to worry about her, I wanted to say, she's nothing to do with us. Her mum will come and fetch her away any day now.

But already this theory was beginning to shake. I'd built it too quickly and carelessly, without any solid ground to support it. Mrs. Martin's marriage did not prove Rosie was not Emma, after all. I mean, kidnappers can get married, can't they?

My grandmother was asking my father what he really thought. "Do you yourself believe the girl is Emma?"

I held my breath.

"I don't know," my father said slowly. "I didn't think so at first. The letter struck me as phony. There was no attempt at proof. No details—the time of day it happened, the shop outside which the pram had been left. Nothing in fact that could not have been lifted straight out of that article in the Sunday paper. And then, sending the child to us on August first—a coincidence, perhaps? I don't altogether trust coincidences."

"What do you mean? I don't understand you, Anthony," my grandmother said.

"The first of August is Emma's birthday."

"Yes. I know that."

"It was never mentioned in the papers, not even after it had first happened. How could that woman have known? You can guess a baby's age to within a week, but surely not to the very day. It looks as if she must have taken the trouble to find out from Somerset House. Rather too calculating, don't you think? It doesn't quite go with that impulsive, tearstained letter. Far more like someone trying deliberately to work on our emotions. And those tearstains! Far too many of them to be convincing."

"Some people do cry a lot," my grandmother said. I wondered if she was thinking of my mother. Or me. "Still, I see what you mean. When was her own baby born—the one she claims has died? Do you know?"

"We think it must be July thirty-first. That's when Rosie says her birthday is. When she's been told it is. And there seems no reason for the woman to have chosen that date otherwise."

"Really, Anthony, for a clever man, you can be very stupid," my grandmother said. "The explanation is right in front of your nose. I doubt if that woman has ever heard of Somerset House. From the letter you showed me, she seems a very simple, uneducated person. Just the type to be sentimental. She simply wanted to spend one last birthday with the child. One more kiss before we part, or one more cake, in this case. Perfectly natural. Besides, she would have needed time to get the child's clothes washed and mended. She wouldn't want her to look neglected. I expect she dressed her up in her Sunday best for the occasion, didn't she?"

"I didn't notice her clothes," my father said slowly. "But you may be right."

(I had noticed her clothes. I remembered the terrible frilly, fussy blouse, the skimpy pink skirt, and the high-heeled shoes. Her best. I imagined her mother saying "Now you want to look nice. It's a posh house you're going to," and Rosie perhaps saying crossly "I'm only delivering a letter, ain't I? What's all the fuss about?")

"And there was the girl herself," my father was saying now. "She looked such a complete stranger. Oh, yes, I know. One could hardly hope to recognize a baby after thirteen years. But I'd have expected some trace of family resemblance, however slight. And I could see none."

"You're wrong, Anthony," Miss Wait said. "There is something . . . only I can't put my finger on it. Resemblance is an odd thing. Like a conjuring trick—now you see it, now you don't. She does remind me of someone. Of course," she added, "it may turn out to be someone on telly, or something like that."

"My eyes are not as sharp as they used to be," my grandmother said. "And I only saw her for a moment. But I don't see why she couldn't be a Seton. In fact, she looks more like a Seton to me than Kate does. Of course, Kate takes after her mother. She's very like Margaret, isn't she?"

"Yes," my father agreed.

Was that why he was disappointed in me? Never seemed to love me as much as I thought he should? I was not a proper Seton. I took after my mother's family, which, as every Seton knew, was inferior. A wishy-washy lot, my mother and me. Given to crying too often. Nervous. No self-control. No stamina.

"By the way, how is Kate taking it all?" Uncle Peter asked, and when my father did not answer (perhaps he was shrugging or making a wry face), he added, "Badly, I expect, knowing Kate." And they all laughed.

That was when I ran away for the second time.

I ran off as stupidly and blindly as if I had still been only five years old. I took nothing with me, no money, no bag, not even a cardigan. I just walked across the hall and let myself quietly out of the front door. This time I did not go down to the corner, but went the other way. Through the posts that separated our street from the heath, where I'd been forbidden ever to go by myself.

I think that's why I chose it. I wanted to show them. I was not dull stay-at-home Kate any longer. I was wild and free and hugely angry.

The heath was deserted. Everyone had hurried home. Dark storm clouds spread over the sky, shadowing the ground, making it look far later than it was. In the distance, a single ray of sunshine pierced the gloom, bathing a tall building in golden radiance, so that it gleamed like a castle in a fairy tale. It was so beautiful that I ran towards it, though I knew I could never reach it. It was miles away, on the other side of the city.

It was still terribly hot and clammy. My clothes stuck to me as I ran. At first my thoughts were hot, too, and childish. I'll show them. They'll be sorry when it's too late. That sort of thing. But soon I was not thinking at all, just running, with my feet thudding over the uneven grass and my eyes fixed on the bright building.

When I stopped for breath, it seemed no nearer. I wondered where it was, in what part of London, for I had lost all sense of direction. Suddenly the ray of sunshine went out and it was a fairy castle no longer, merely a high building like a dirty finger poking the sky. For all I knew it might have been an office block in Hockley. Dismal, dirty Hockley, that for Rosie would always be bathed in sunlight, because it was her old home.

I stood there, feeling for the first time lost and a little frightened, with no bright point to run towards any longer, only the gray smudged horizon in front of me and the empty grass all around. The first thunder rolled above my head. Fat, lukewarm drops fell from the sky, slowly at first, and then faster and faster, soaking me to the skin.

I didn't care. I wanted to catch pneumonia and die. They'd be sorry then.

It was no good. My anger had cooled and I sounded silly, even to myself. A sudden white glare of lightning lit the heath like a stage. I was the only person there. The audience had all stayed at home.

I was frightened of the thunder, and the trees wincing under the lash of the rain and the quick, cold burn of electricity in the dark sky. I turned and ran back the way I had come. Over the wet grass, over the wet pavement, slipping and skidding, blinded by the rain in my eyes.

I crashed right into him.

He was standing outside our house, a large, looming man, with huge shoulders and a round red face fringed by wet hair. I squeaked in terror and would have fallen, had he not held me up with enormous hairy hands.

"Steady on, lass. Look where you're going. You nearly had us both over."

His breath was warm and beery, like a pub. I could see the rain running down his face, trickling through the curly hairs on his chin. "Got caught in the storm? You'd better hurry home, hadn't you?"

"Yes. Thank you."

He let me go and I put my hand on the gate.

"Is this where you live?" he asked with interest.

"Yes."

"I thought another little girl lived in this house. A little girl with dark hair. A skinny little girl."

"That's Rosie. Do you know her? Have you come for her?"

"No, no! No, the little girl I was looking for isn't called Rosie. Betty. That's her name, Betty. Sorry, lass, I must have the wrong address." Without another word, he turned and hurried off into the rain. I heard an engine start up. A van pulled away from the pavement and was soon out of sight.

I stared after him. Then I ran into the house.

No one had even missed me. When I came through the back door, I found my mother in the kitchen, searching through the deep freeze.

"Mummy," I cried. "There was a—"

"Kate!" she interrupted, staring. "You're soaking wet. Where have you been?"

"Just in the garden. Mummy, listen, there was—"

"You are a little idiot. Go and change at once. Look at the mess you're making on the floor."

"Mummy, I want to tell you something. There was this funny man—"

"Not now, darling. I haven't time to listen to jokes. I'm terribly busy. They're staying to supper. All of them. I had to ask them, but I hoped they'd refuse. They did refuse at first, but your father said, nonsense, it was no trouble at all. We had plenty of food. I suppose we have. But none of it seems to match. Chicken Chasseur for Two. Three Rainbow Trouts. Beef Casserole. Something without a label. I suppose I could mix them all together and hope for the best. Kate, do go and change, there's an angel. And you might take this milk up to Rosie. She's got a tummy ache, poor child, so I've put her to bed. She wanted to see you. Said she had something to tell you."

"What?"

"I don't know. She wouldn't tell me. Said it was a secret."

I walked slowly upstairs, thinking hard about the man in the rain. He had meant Rosie, all right. I was sure of that, whatever he had said. Why had he rushed off like that? Who was he? I should have asked his name, invited him in to see my father. I should have stopped him from going, somehow, or at least got the number of his van. I should never have let him vanish into the rain. He might be the one person who could have told us where Rosie's mum was now. . . .

Water from my wet hair ran down the back of my neck, and I shivered. What could I tell them? Just— there was this funny man. Somehow I did not think they would be amused. I wondered if it was necessary to mention it at all.

17

"You washed your hair?" Rosie asked. She was sitting up in bed, her face flushed, trying to look as if she hadn't just thrust something under her pillow as I came in.

"No. I went for a walk."

"In all the wet?"

"I was running away."

She stared at me. "You ain't serious?"

"No. It was a joke. Here's your milk."

"Ta." She took the mug from me and balanced it on her knee. "I nearly run away once," she said. "Got my bags packed and everything. Then I thought—where the hell am I going? Nowhere. So I hid out on Hockley Station, down on the platform, just to make Mum worried. I meant to stay out late, but it was draughty and there were drunks, and I'd finished my book, so I went back. She was still out so she never knew nothing. Just as well. She'd have been worried sick." She broke off, looking puzzled, then added, "She would, you know."

"Mummy would cry her eyes out if I ran away," I said. "She'd probably have a nervous breakdown." It sounded like boasting. Luckily Rosie did not seem to be listening. She had put her milk down on the table and was fumbling under the pillow, bringing out something she kept concealed in her hand.

"If I show you something, you won't tell, will you?"

"No. I promise."

I had guessed what it was. I was not surprised when she opened her hand to see the small crumpled square of blue paper.

"It's a letter from my mum," she said, unfolding it

carefully. The paper was limp now and looked as if it would tear easily. "It ain't to me, it's to one of her friends. Bettine. She works at the launderette and she give it to me. Mum's got married."

I did not tell her that I already knew this. "Married? Has she? Who to?"

"She don't say. Ain't put no address, neither. D'you want to see it? Here." She passed it to me, warning me to be careful and not tear it.

The same blue ink, hardly darker than the bright blue paper. The same round, unsteady hand. No capitals or commas or periods made it difficult to understand.

dear bettine,
   i am sorry i went off without saying goodbye but i wos in a state i had to give rosie back to her peeple you see she wos never my baby reely i wos just minding her i had no choice it wos only rite now for the good news i am married he is a good man and erns good money and he ses he will take care of me it wos a quiet wedding i wish you had bin there but we dint have nobody i wos crying and my maskara run i bet i look orful but he sed i look luvly he bort me a bowkay pink roses in silver paper ever so pretty i wish i coud send it her but better not it is my cross i put it in my fridje and he ses it will keep fresh like on the day we got a luvly flat i miss hockley and the green man we had good times dint we? he ses i will get over it but it is bound to take time he is ever so kind

all the best from your frend
Louise

I sat holding the letter. My heart was beating very quickly. Outside the window thunder roared in the sky and the rain fell heavily, shutting us in.

"What d'you think?" Rosie asked. Her face was anxious. I did not know what to say. "D'you think she was crying about me?"

I looked at her blankly. "Crying? I didn't notice—"

"Yeh. There, see?" She pointed: "i wos crying and my maskara run."

People do cry at weddings, I thought. Not the bride, perhaps.

"Look, she wanted to send me her bouquet. I wish she had. It'd be something . . . something to . . ."

"Rosie, don't—"

"I ain't crying. I ain't crying over *her.*"

I looked down at the letter again. When I'd first read it, the words about giving Rosie back to her people had jumped out at me, and I had read on quickly, hardly taking anything else in.

But Rosie must have read it over and over again, searching for crumbs of comfort like a bird in winter. Now I saw what she had found, the small glints of unhappiness, like tears falling behind the bridal veil: "i wos in a state . . . i had no choice . . . it wos only rite . . . it is my cross."

I wondered if Sundays still made Rosie's mum feel bad, or if she had found some sort of peace now that she had given Rosie back to us—

Emma. Not Rosie, *Emma.* My sister?

I looked up and saw she was watching me. Perhaps waiting for me to say it aloud. I tried to, honestly, but somehow I couldn't.

"Mum's a terrible liar, you know," she said, still watching me. "She'll say anything that suits her. It don't mean it's true. She's made up of lies—even her

own name. You know what your dad thinks? That it
ain't really Martin at all and that's why he couldn't find
no record. You don't want to believe a word she says."
She took back the letter from me and pointed. "Look,
there's a lie right there. Making out she's a child
minder."

"I suppose she couldn't very well say that . . ."

"That she stole me out of your mum's pram?"

"Yes."

"D'you think it's true, then?"

"It might be."

"Might be!" she shouted. "That ain't good enough.
I want to *know*."

There was a crash of thunder and we both looked
at the window. The rain was falling straight down, like
the bars of a silver cage.

"I can't be Emma. I can't. I been Rosie too long."
Her voice was rising. "I'll always be Rosie," she said,
thumping her chest.

"We could go on calling you Rosie. I'm sure
Mummy wouldn't mind."

"Oh, Gawd, you're such a kid. I didn't mean. . . .
I dunno what I meant. It's like . . . I can't be somebody's lost baby. I been a baby. I done all that with
Mum. Cut my teeth, had chicken pox and measles, fell
off my friend's bike, the lot. I'm thirteen now, that's
nearly grown up. I can't change back just to suit your
mum. And it's not as if the rest of you wanted me."

"How do you mean?"

"I ain't stupid. Your dad's been kind and all that,
but he won't never be happy not knowing. Every time I
do something wrong, he'll be thinking, 'She ain't one of
us.' And your Mrs. Trapp don't fool me with her
'dearies.' She couldn't find her purse last week and you
should've seen the way she looked at me. 'You haven't

seen it, have you, dearie? I know I put it on the table and it's not there now.' And all the time it was in her shopping bag. She thinks I'm a thief. She's always watching me. She nearly wets her pants when I go near them silver candlesticks on the sideboard. And as for you—"

"What about me?"

"You're a bleeding little snob, ain't you?"

"I'm not!"

She shrugged, "Oh, you ain't said nothing. But I seen the look on your face, like I was a bad smell."

"That's not fair. I've been jolly kind to you."

"Kind!" she shouted. "Yeh, you've all been *kind*, and I hope it chokes you."

A flash of lightning flooded the room, washing all the color from it. Everything was black and white. Suddenly I saw again the face of the boy in the photograph, the face I had destroyed. The eyes stared out boldly from beneath straight black brows, the dark hair fell in spikes over the forehead. There it was, the resemblance they were all looking for. Then it was gone again, and it was Rosie sitting staring at me angrily, as if she knew what I had done.

I don't care, I thought.

A clap of thunder, like a giant smack from God, rattled the windows, and I jumped in terror.

"You're not frightened of thunder, are you?" Rosie asked.

"A bit."

"I'm not."

"You're frightened of dogs," I muttered.

"Yeh. And spiders and ghosts. I wasn't making myself out a hero. I just like thunder. It's wild. All that flashing and banging, like fireworks, only for free. It makes me want to clap and shout back."

"I just want to hide."

"Like my mum. She hates it. She used to shut her eyes and put her fingers in her ears, like someone up there was shouting at her. 'Guilty conscience,' I'd tell her, 'that's your trouble.' Hey, that was a big bang. Kate, it's all right, silly. It can't hurt you, you know."

I was trembling. "The lightning can," I said. "It can strike you dead."

"Not indoors. It can't reach us in here."

I wished I could be certain. The flickering light and the thunderclaps, coming closer and closer, terrified me. I kept seeing Rosie's face changing into the photograph and back again. I thought I was going mad.

"Cheer up, kid. It'll soon be over. Your hair's drying rough. I'll brush it for you."

I passed her the hairbrush from the dressing table. Kneeling up in bed, she began brushing my hair, like someone stroking a pony to quiet it.

"It's still a bit damp. You must've got soaked. There, that's better." She put the brush down and glanced at me out of the corner of her eye. "Was you really trying to run away?"

"Not really. I just wanted to be out on my own for a bit."

"Yeh. I know." Rosie turned and looked out of the window, and sighed. The storm had passed overhead. Already the lightning was less bright and the thunder lagged behind. I think she was sorry to see it go. She sat back at last and began folding the letter, very carefully, over and over into a small square.

"I wish I knew 'oo she's married," she said. "I didn't think she had no new boyfriend. She never spoke of one. . . . If she's married that fat pig, I'll kill her."

"Who?"

"That Harry Jenkins. Remember, I told you about him."

"The one who got drunk?"

"Yeh. And broke her bingo vase."

"I thought you said she'd thrown him out."

"I only hope she threw him far enough," Rosie muttered.

I was silent for a moment. Then I asked uneasily, "What does he look like?"

"Horrible," Rosie said. "Huge. Fat. Hairy. Like a blooming red ape."

(A wet ape, a huge dripping shadow who'd loomed out of the rain looking for her—"I thought another little girl lived in this house. A little girl with dark hair. A skinny little girl." "That's Rosie," I'd said. "Do you know her? Have you come for her?")

I shivered. "I think I've seen him," I said slowly. "I think he's looking for you—"

"Him? Harry Jenkins? You're dreaming, kid. If he's married Mum, he won't want me hanging around. He knows what I think of him. If he's married Mum . . ." She lay back suddenly and turned her face to the pillow.

I felt awkward. I wished I hadn't mentioned the man at the gate.

"I ought to be going down," I said at last. "I promised Mummy I'd lay the table. Is there anything I can get you?"

"No, ta very—I mean, thanks most awfully."

"I don't mean to be a snob!" I burst out.

"No. Sorry. It ain't your fault."

I opened the door. From downstairs the sound of voices reached us. Someone laughed loudly. Miss Wait, I thought.

"They don't know what it's like, do they?" Rosie

said. "They don't know what it's like for us. You and me, we're right in the middle of it. They think it's their problem, but it ain't. It's ours."

18

Outside, the storm had gone and it was much cooler. A fine rain fell for three days, keeping us out of the garden. Rosie no longer sat on the front wall, looking for her mum. Yet somehow the thunder and lightning seemed to linger in our house, rumbling in dark corners or flaring out in little quarrels.

Rosie began behaving badly. She swore at my father. She refused to leave her room when my grandmother called again to see her. My father lost his temper, a thing he hardly ever does, and shouted at her. She shouted back.

Mummy and Daddy quarreled. They pretended they hadn't, but they couldn't fool me. I knew. I'd heard the sounds coming through their closed door; the high mewing and the low growling, like a cat and dog hating each other.

Then my mother shouted at Mrs. Trapp and Mrs. Trapp gave in her notice. My mother burst into tears. Mrs. Trapp agreed to stay after all. But the next day Rosie threw a doughnut at Mrs. Trapp. I forget why. It hit her on the cheek and at the sight of her face, purple with anger and speckled with sugar like a crystalized plum, I could not help laughing out loud. Mrs. Trapp gave in her notice again. My mother cried even louder. Mrs. Trapp weakened.

"If she apologizes," she said. "I'll stay."

"I'm sorry. Honestly. I didn't mean to laugh. It was shock or something."

"I didn't mean you, Kate. That other one," she said, as if she could not bring herself to soil her lips with Rosie's name.

" 'Oo d'you think you're talking about? I got a name, ain't I?" Rosie shouted. Then her face seemed to come to pieces like a torn photograph. "No, you're right! I ain't got a name no more. I'm nobody, that's 'oo I am. Nobody. Well, then, Nobody apologizes to you. Nobody's sorry they hit you. Will that do, you fat pig?"

"Rosie—" my mother began, but Rosie screamed at her, "Don't call me that! Don't call me anything! I hate the lot of you!"

She did apologize in the end, however (if you call a mumbled "Mr.-Seton-says-I-got-to-say-I'm-sorry" an apology and not merely reporting). Mrs. Trapp chose to accept it, though she made it quite clear it was only for my mother's sake. "Poor Mrs. Seton has enough to put up with as it is," she said.

I was the good one now. I got no credit for it. At first I tried helpful remarks. Like—"I know it's hard for you, Rosie, but you might think of Mummy. It isn't easy for her either, you know." This pleased no one, not even my mother. You can't win, can you? In the end, I gave up trying and just watched and listened.

We went on, bumping unevenly from day to day, each outburst followed by a period of uneasy quiet. No one spoke about finding Rosie's mum anymore, not even Rosie. Once when I tried to talk about her mother, she shouted at me to shut up. "I don't want to talk about her. I don't want to think about her. I don't want to see her, not ever again," she said.

What are you going to do, then? I wanted to ask.

Stay with us? But I did not say it aloud. Even I could see she was terribly unhappy.

Sometimes she would seem to cheer up a little. I'd find her looking round our home thoughtfully, as if wondering what it would be like to live here always. She'd study my parents' faces, when she thought herself unobserved, and then glance in a mirror. Once, when I came into the sitting room unexpectedly (for I walk very quietly), I found her with a silver frame in her hand, which she put down quickly on the table. It held a photograph of me, wearing skis and a silly grin— I think I'd just picked myself up from the snow.

"That was taken in Switzerland," I said. "The year before last."

"Dunno how you manage them things."

"It's quite easy. I could show you. I expect we'll be going again this winter." I said it deliberately, wanting to see what she'd say.

Nothing. She just looked at me in silence, then gave an awkward little smile and turned away.

No one bothered to tell me what we were going to do if we never found her mum. I suppose I could have asked. I don't quite know why I didn't. Perhaps because I thought I knew the answer: we would keep her. I'd have to be a younger sister. I'd have to take second place.

I wasn't certain how I felt about it now. You see, I'd begun to like Rosie. I don't know when it started. Possibly the day in Hockley, when she'd screamed at that woman and lifted her skirt to show the crowd she hadn't a bruise on her. I'd been embarrassed at the time. Now, looking back, it seemed funny. I could imagine us saying, when we were quite old, "Do you remember that day in the market?" and laughing together. And there was the night in the storm, when she had brushed my hair to soothe me, when she had said, "You and me, we're right in the middle of it," and I'd had a glimpse of what it might be like to have a sister at home, when the grown-ups were talking importantly downstairs, shutting us out. It might be fun having a sister like Rosie . . . if only she'd be happy. It wasn't much fun at the moment with her glooming around and everyone else having to walk on eggshells.

It was getting us all down, especially my mother. She's always been a bit twitchy; now she was worse than ever. She no longer went to her painting classes or drama group or bridge club, but stayed at home and worried. She used to hover over us, like a damp cloud. I think she was afraid to take her eyes off Rosie in case she vanished as suddenly as she had appeared. And there was always a silly, anxious smile on her face: it made me want to shake her.

"Why don't you leave Rosie alone, Mummy?" I asked. "You only make her worse. She hates to be fussed over, anyone can see that."

"I expect you're right," my mother said after a pause, turning away. "After all, you know her better than I do."

I had hurt her, but I didn't know what to do about it. What I'd said was true. She did get on Rosie's nerves. Come to that, she got on mine too. At least now she gave up following us everywhere, asking us what we would like to do, and suggesting silly things like visits to museums and art galleries, and being snubbed by Rosie for her pains. Instead she retreated to the back bedroom she called her studio. Often when we were in the garden, we'd see her standing by her easel in the open window, painting the view that included us.

One day Rosie, seeing her there, muttered something under her breath. I thought it was probably something rude and said sharply, "What did you say?"

"I said I think I'm gonna go mad."

That night I had a horrible dream. I dreamed of three boys on a windy beach. One of them had black hair blowing across his forehead.

"Robbie," I said.

"Don't call me that. I'm not Robbie. I'm nobody. Nobody," he cried. "Help me. I'm frightened. I want to *know.*"

Then I saw it wasn't a boy at all. It was Rosie. She was staring at me, her hair whipping about her head in small black snakes. The wind was tearing her to pieces. "Help me," she cried, but I could not move. I saw her face split. I watched helplessly as she broke into fragments before my eyes; torn pieces of paper whirling out to sea.

"Emma! Emma, come back!" I shouted, but it was too late. She had vanished into the tumbling water and was gone.

The dream stuck to me. In the daytime it was no more than a small shadow clinging to my heels. After all, I hadn't murdered anyone. I'd torn up a photograph, that's hardly a major crime. But at night the shadow grew, joining the other darknesses round my bed. Then I felt horribly guilty.

Odd bits of talk I'd overheard on my silent rambles through the house came back to haunt me—"done my best to reassure her, but I doubt if Rosie will ever be happy unless she knows . . . feels utterly lost . . . seriously worried about her . . ."

My mother's voice, high-pitched, coming from behind their closed door—"Proof! Proof! Why do you always need proof? She *must* be Emma—do you think I

want to go on blaming myself for the rest of my life?
. . . It's no good saying it wasn't my fault. It was! It was!
If only I'd taken better care of her, if only I hadn't left
her outside the shop . . ."

Tossing and turning on my bed, I felt the whole
weight of our unhappy home pressing down on me. My
father's steps coming up to bed sounded like those of an
old and defeated man. The wind was my mother crying. The silence in Rosie's room seemed to shout "Nobody. Nobody's in here."

What a fuss over one photograph? I suppose so. I
told myself so. After all, surely there must be other
photographs of Robbie somewhere.

"Mummy, you know Cousin Robbie?" I asked next
morning.

"Robbie? Robbie? I don't remember a Robbie. But
your father has so many cousins. I can't possibly remember them all. What about him?"

"Oh, nothing. It doesn't matter."

"Why don't you ask Daddy?"

But asking my father was more tricky. He was
sharper than my mother, full of questions and curiosity.
Guilt made me feel transparent. I was afraid he would
take one look through me and know what I had done.

I went into his study before supper. He was looking
through some papers on his desk. He always brought
work home from the office. It made it difficult to talk to
him. It was like having to shout at a deaf person; you felt
you had to have something important to say.

"Are you busy, Daddy?"

"Well"—he glanced at his desk, then swiveled his
chair round to face me—"no, these can wait a minute.
What is it, Kate?"

"I just wondered. . . . You know Cousin Robbie?"

"Robbie? Robert Seton? Good Lord, I haven't seen him in years." He paused. I waited, hoping he would say, "Of course! That's who Rosie reminds me of. She's the very image of Robbie Seton." Then I would have made up for what I had done, and there'd be no need to confess or anything impossible like that. But he did not. He merely looked puzzled and said, "What's all this about Robbie, Kate? Why the sudden interest? You've never even met him."

"Miss Wait was talking about him the other day," I lied.

"Was she? Don't tell me she's kept in touch with him all this time?"

"No. It was about when you were children."

"What was she saying about him?"

"Oh, um—just that she liked him best of all her cousins."

"Did she indeed?" he said, smiling. "And I always thought I was her favorite."

"You?" I asked, astonished. "Did she want to marry you? Is that why Mummy doesn't like her?"

"No. For heaven's sake, Kate, I was only joking. And I don't know what gave you the idea that your mother doesn't like her. Of course she does. She's very fond of her."

He must be blind, I thought. Mummy can't stand her.

"What was Miss Wait like when she was young?" I asked.

"Oh, she was a jolly sort of girl. Good at games. Good with animals. I'm very fond of Elizabeth. I've known her all my life. But if you're imagining some sort of childhood romance between us, I'm afraid I must disappoint you. She loved horses and dogs. I loved cars and cricket. We were very young for our age."

I remembered the old photographs in the album. Miss Wait—the square girl with thick legs and thin plaits. My father, a smiling boy with curly hair—had she secretly loved him? Or had she loved the black-eyed, black-haired Robbie Seton? I don't suppose either of them paid much attention to her. For a moment, the shadows of the past children moved in my thoughts, playing the old triangle game, in which one is always left out.

"I suppose she wasn't very pretty," I said.

He had gone back to his paper. "Mmm?"

"Miss Wait. Are there any old photographs of her?"

"There are one or two in the family album. I was looking through it the other day, as it happens. And there should be a lot more in a cardboard box somewhere. You could try the attic." He was looking at me again, his papers forgotten for the moment. "Why are you so interested in them, Kate?"

"It's funny to think of you as children. I just wanted to see what you looked like."

He smiled, but I don't think he believed me, because he said thoughtfully, "Robbie had black hair, I remember. A thin, dark boy. If you find any photographs of him, Kate, let me see them, will you?"

"All right."

"Good girl."

He was pleased with me. He thought I was trying to help. He had no idea I was only trying to make up for what I had done.

I left searching the attic till the following morning, when my father was at work and my mother had taken Rosie to the dentist for a checkup. There were dozens of cardboard boxes of all sizes, some done up with string, some with an elastic band. Old clothes, old let-

ters, old theater programs. I was firm with myself. I had
not very much time. Rosie and my mother would be
back for lunch.

They were in the tenth box I opened; hundreds of
photographs, some old, some new, all jumbled up together. I took them down to my room and started sort-
ing them out; grandparents, uncles, cousins and aunts,
babies and kittens, horses and houses. . . . I did not
find any photographs of Cousin Robbie. What I did find
were five of my sister Emma.

19

Small babies are much the same, aren't they? At first I
thought they were all me, and put them on one side,
meaning to look at them later, with the interest you
can't help feeling in old photographs of yourself.

By chance, two of them slipped off the bed, landing
face up on the floor, side by side. Each showed a baby in
its pram beneath our elderberry tree. The babies
looked identical; both fast asleep, their eyelids creased
between little bunches of fat and their soft mouths
open. The prams were different.

One was large and black and very shiny. The other
was pale blue and smaller. Two prams: two babies. One
of them was Emma.

She was in the black pram, and I was in the blue. I
was sure of this because we had given my pram to Mrs.
Trapp's niece after I had grown out of it. For years I had
seen it being wheeled down Heath Street, its blue getting shabbier and shabbier, like a city sky. Looking at
Emma in her glossy pram, I felt a prick of jealousy that
hers should have been so much grander than mine.

Silly, wasn't it? I don't know why my mother had not kept it for me. Perhaps with Emma gone, she could not bear the sight of it anymore.

I looked more closely at the other photographs. There were two of Miss Wait, standing outside St. Peter's, holding a baby in a long, embroidered gown. In one, the bush beside the porch was in full leaf. The other showed bare winter twigs. The button-nosed babies might have been anyone, but they weren't. They were Emma and me, wearing in turn the dress that our grandmother had been christened in.

Here was a close-up of Emma in her black pram. Her eyes were open and looked dark. She had no hair. In one hand she was gripping the arm of a knitted toy, a teddy bear. It was white and had a pink ribbon round its neck. It was in the other photographs too, half hidden by blankets or half lost in shadows.

I had had a pram toy, a brown velvet mouse called Tappy. When I was small, he went with me everywhere. I would not go to sleep without him in my cot. I screamed if anyone tried to take him away. Emma held her toy very tightly. If I'd been going to steal her from her pram, I'd have taken baby, blanket, teddy, and all.

I sat looking at the photograph, and I began to see how I could put things right.

There was a row that evening. My father told Rosie he had made an appointment for her to see Miss Bowman, the headmistress of my school. He was hoping she'd be able to start there in September.

Rosie stared. Her? Go to a snob school? He must be joking. She was staying at her old school, she said. Where her friends were.

My father pointed out that it was well over an

hour's journey to Hockley—"You'd be tired before you got there."

"I wouldn't. I'm tough. Not like some people." (She meant me, I suppose.)

"You'd like it at Queen Charlotte's, Rosie," my mother said. "You'd soon make new friends. It's a very friendly school, isn't it, Kate?"

"Yes."

Rosie heard the doubt in my voice. "Sounds enthusiastic, don't she? I ain't seen none of her friends round here. You sure she's got any?"

"Of course I have! Lots!"

"Yeh? You could've fooled me."

"My best friend's still away—" I began, then saw my father was watching me, his eyes very cold. "But I was going to ask some of the others to tea next week." He looked away, satisfied.

Rosie, however, wasn't grateful.

"Remind me to have a bath and mend my panties," she said. "Mustn't disgrace you."

I ignored this and went out of the room, thinking I might as well telephone my friends now and get it over with. Before I shut the door behind me, I heard Rosie tell my father, "If I can't stay at my old school, I ain't stopping here. I'll run away."

Nobody asked her where she thought she could go.

None of my friends could come next week. I'd made excuses for too long. I could tell from their voices that they wanted to show me they could get along without me very well. They couldn't come next week, and they weren't any too certain about the following week either. "You're not the only one who's too busy," I was told.

At last I managed to persuade three of them to

come. Not next Wednesday, but the one after that. It seemed a long way away. They were not girls I particularly liked, but they were part of the crowd I went around with at school. I did not tell them about Rosie. Perhaps they would have come sooner if I had, out of curiosity, but I did not know what to say.

The next day it was raining and much colder. My mother said she would take us shopping and buy us some new clothes. I think she hoped Rosie would be pleased. She wasn't.

"I don't want none," she said.

"But, Rosie, darling, you haven't anything warm—"

"I ain't cold." Goosepimples were standing out on her thin arms.

"I thought a cardigan—"

"I hate cardigans. I ain't going to be dressed up like a prize pig just for her snobby friends."

I was furious with her. "You are a bitch," I said.

My mother told me to apologize at once. I refused.

"It was my fault," Rosie said quickly. "The kid's right. I was being bitchy. I dunno what comes over me."

My mother's face was soft. "I know, darling," she said. "I understand."

I was fed up with everyone having to be sorry for Rosie. The sooner my plan worked, the better.

"I want to go shopping," I said loudly.

The store was hot and crowded. I got lost.

"Where did you get to?" my mother asked.

"I went to the Ladies," I said. "I don't know why you made such a fuss. I wasn't gone more than half an hour."

"It was much longer than that. You should have

told me where you were going. We've been looking for you everywhere."

Rosie was watching us. Her face was expressionless.

"Thought you'd been stolen away," she said. "Like Emma."

"Well, I've come back now," I said sharply. "Like you."

That shut her up. My mother frowned at me.

We were outside the store now. It had stopped raining. We walked down to the corner in the watery sunlight, looking for a taxi. I was happy. Pinned inside my loose dress and bumping against my bottom was a plastic bag. My private shopping. I had got lost on purpose.

This is what I had bought:
2 oz. white wool
1/2 yard pink ribbon
knitting needles size 8
pattern no. 27563
The pattern was for a teddy bear. It was exactly like, as far as I could tell, the one in the photograph.

I was going to make the bear. I was going to dirty it, pull it about, tear it here and there until it looked thirteen years old. Then I was going to wrap it up and post it to Miss Emma Seton at our address.

One morning soon, it would arrive like something out of the past: the toy Emma had been holding when she was stolen from her pram, the proof everyone was looking for.

Then perhaps I could stop dreaming of a torn photograph blowing into the sea. Rosie would no longer lie awake in the cold moonlight, hearing the owls cry "Who? Who?" I would have given her a name, Emma Seton, and only I would ever know that it might not be the right one. I said I was happy, but perhaps excited was more the word. I had a secret now. One that I would have to keep till the end of my life.

Knitting away behind my locked door, I could hear Rosie pacing restlessly, endlessly, about the house. Sometimes her voice would be raised in shrill anger downstairs. Sometimes I thought I heard her crying in her room at night. I told myself she'll have to wait. It was only for a short time. I could finish it in a week, if people would only stop bothering me. Mostly I knitted late at night, trying to keep my eyes open and failing, dropping stitches like crumbs into my bed. Whenever my mother was out and Mrs. Trapp busy downstairs, I locked myself into my room. The first time, there was a soft knock at my door.

"Who is it?" I demanded irritably, although I knew it must be Rosie.

"It's only me."

"What do you want now?" I sounded unfriendly, for I wanted to get on with my knitting.

Silence. Then she said in a flat voice, "Nothing. It don't matter."

I heard the sound of her footsteps going away. She must have been desperately lonely, but she never knocked on my door again. Secrets are dangerous. They shut people out.

20

On Wednesday the weather changed for the better. It was the only thing that did. From my bedroom window I could see Rosie in the garden. She was sitting on the swing, going backwards and forwards, higher and higher, as if she wanted to kick the sun out of the sky. Mrs. Trapp was in the kitchen and a warm smell of baking filled the house. It was the day my friends were coming to tea.

I sighed. It was too soon. The teddy bear, wrapped up and ready, was hidden on the top shelf of my wardrobe. I hadn't had a chance to post it. Rosie was still swinging backwards and forwards; Rosie or Emma, Emma or Rosie. It was all she wanted to do nowadays. Whenever the sun shone, you'd find her in the garden, going backwards and forwards until the sound of the chain squeaking made you want to scream. It is difficult to talk to someone on a swing. Perhaps that's why she did it. She never spoke to me now unless she had to. When it rained she shut herself in her room, and never answered when I knocked and called her name.

"Where's Rosie?" my mother would ask when I came downstairs without her.

"In her room. She wants to be by herself."

It was never any good. My mother always went up to see if Rosie was all right, though I knew she'd only get hurt. I'd stand on the bottom step listening, and hear her knock on the door. "Rosie?" and then again when there was no answer, "Rosie, my dear, may I come in?"

Yes, go in, I'd think. Tell her to stop behaving like a brat. Shake some sense into her.

But I knew she would not. She'd say something in a soft, ingratiating voice, like a timid dog wagging its tail to show it didn't want a fight. Rosie would snap and snarl at her, and my mother would come down again, slowly, not knowing what to do.

Seeing her weak, worried face, I'd want to scream "Don't be so feeble! Do something. You're the grown-up." Then I'd notice the skin puckering round her eyes, and afraid she'd decide to have one of her migraines, I'd say quickly, "Don't worry, Mummy. She'll be all right." I hated it when she shut herself away from us in a darkened room. Miss Wait had planted a maggot in my mind that day on the heath when she'd suggested it must be easier to have a nervous breakdown and lie in bed crying than to face all the troubles outside.

Things must have improved between my mother and Rosie, however. They must have actually had a conversation together without my noticing. For that morning my mother told me Rosie had agreed to come to my tea party.

"Has she? When did she say so?" I asked.

"Yesterday." My mother was in her bedroom, sitting in front of her mirror, her hairbrush in her hand. "I have three gray hairs," she said.

"They don't show."

"I pulled them out. Kate, about this afternoon . . ."

"That's what I wanted to ask you about. How am I supposed to introduce Rosie? I mean, who shall I say she is?"

She frowned. "Haven't you told your friends about her?"

"No."

"I see."

I wondered uneasily what she saw. Me in a bad light probably.

"*You've* never said it in so many words," I pointed out. "When your friends come, you never say 'This is our daughter Emma.' You just say 'This is Rosie,' and leave it at that. And you're lucky. Your friends never ask awkward questions. Mine will."

She was silent.

"I'll do whatever you want," I said. "If you want me

to say 'This is my long-lost sister Emma,' I will. But you
know what would happen? Rosie will start screaming 'I
ain't Emma! I'm nobody! I hate you!' "

"Kate!"

"She would. You know she would. She always
does."

My mother sighed. "Perhaps we were wrong. I
don't know. Perhaps we should have insisted right from
the beginning that she was Emma. . . . Only she got
so upset. Your father thought—we both thought—it was
better to take things slowly. We didn't want to frighten
her away."

She made Rosie sound like a wild animal they were
approaching on tiptoe, hoping that sooner or later she
would let them come near enough to let them slip a
collar on.

"I'm beginning to think it was a mistake to try and
trace Mrs. Martin," she went on. "Those detectives—
it's not as if they've been any good. And it may have
given Rosie the idea that we didn't want her, whatever
we said. But your father thought it was important to
know . . . I mean, I expect he thought she might settle
down more quickly if . . . well, if . . ."

"If there was some proof?"

"Only to convince her," my mother said hastily.
"I'm perfectly satisfied."

"Satisfied?"

"That she's Emma."

"Why?"

She had not expected the question and it flustered
her. Her hand went up to her forehead as if brushing
away a web of possible lies too tangled to be of any use.

"Oh, for many reasons. Little things . . . I can't
put it into words. Your father will be able to explain it
better than I can," she added hopefully.

Our eyes met in the mirror and she looked quickly away. She isn't sure, she just wants to be, I thought. I couldn't help feeling pleased. I'd have hated all my effort to be wasted.

"What do you want me to do, then?"

"Let me think. . . . Who did you say was coming?"

"Susan Featherstone, Diana Winters, and Charlotte Hepworth."

"Do I know them? Have they been here before?"

"No. My friends—I mean my other friends—couldn't come. You've seen Susan, though. She's the fat one with red cheeks who was the Dutch doll in the school play. Her mother was organizing the teas. The bossy one. In a green dress."

"Oh, yes, I remember now." She hesitated, looking at a loss, then said at last, "I think you'd better have a word with them before they come. You could ring them and say . . ."

"Say what?"

"I'm trying to think. Well, I should tell them about Rosie, say how excited we all are, how wonderful it is to have her back. But explain she's going through a difficult time and ask them not to . . . not to . . ."

"Be horrid to her?"

"No, of course not. Why should they be? I'm sure they're very nice children. Just warn them not to ask any questions that might embarrass her. I'm sure they'll understand. Children are very kind."

I was silent, thinking about Charlotte and Diana and Susan. I knew children could be very cruel.

"I don't want to do it," I said. "*You* ring them."

I could see she didn't want to either. We are very alike in some ways.

"They'd take more notice of you," I said. "You

could talk to their mothers. It's your job. You're the grown-up. You're supposed to look after us." I didn't care then if I hurt her. I was angry at the way she tried to slide out of things.

But to my surprise she agreed and said, "Cheer up, darling. I'm sure it will be a lovely party."

"Do you think Rosie really will come down?"

"Oh, yes. She promised me she would," my mother said with unusual confidence. "You know, I believe she is beginning to accept us at last. She let me buy her those dresses the other day. It's the first time she's ever let me give her anything."

My friends arrived all together at three o'clock. Susan's mother had driven them over, and she came in to arrange about collecting them. At least, that was her excuse. She was bulging with curiosity and determined to get my mother alone, so I took the three girls out into the garden.

They looked round, inquisitive as sparrows, and not seeing Rosie anywhere, crowded round me, all talking at once.

"Where is she?"

"Is she really your sister?"

"Why didn't you tell us?"

"What's she like?"

"Sh-hh," I said, glancing uneasily at Rosie's open window. They looked up too.

"Is that her room?" Susan whispered.

"Yes."

"Isn't she coming down?"

"Yes. She's just getting ready."

"Do you think she heard us?"

"It wouldn't matter if she did," Charlotte said. She was a tall girl, thin and clever. "We didn't say anything horrid. Personally I think the worst thing we can do is whisper. She's bound to guess it's about her."

We all realized this was true. Silence.

"What are we supposed to talk about?" Susan said, and giggled.

"Holidays," Charlotte said.

"Where did you go for your holidays?" I asked obediently.

We were still talking, in loud, self-conscious voices, about Greece and France and Spain, when my mother joined us.

"Where's Rosie?" she asked at once.

"I think she's still in her room getting ready."

"I should go and bring her down, darling. She may be feeling a little shy."

I found Rosie in the sitting room. I wondered how long she had been standing there, watching us through the open windows. She was wearing the dreadful frilly blouse, tight skirt, and tatty high-heeled shoes she had worn when she first came to us. Her face was made up; bright blue eyeshadow and ice-pale lipstick, and her black hair was all stiff and spiky again.

"Why aren't you wearing one of your new dresses?" I asked, before I could stop myself.

Her face went sullen. "Why should I?"

"Mummy was so pleased . . . Oh, never mind."

"I did try them on," she muttered, half in apology. "But . . . I dunno. I didn't look like me anymore."

I wanted to say she might have thought of that before she let Mummy buy them for her, but I didn't. I could tell that, for all her brave war paint, she was nervous.

"It doesn't matter," I said. "You look fine. Come on."

It seemed a long walk over the grass. Everyone stared.

Then my mother came towards us, put her arm round Rosie, and said, "Hullo, darling, come and meet Kate's little friends"—as if by shrinking us she could make Rosie feel better.

I saw Susan nudge Diana, and Diana put her hand over her mouth to hide a smile. After my mother had made the introductions, there was one of those silences that seem to suck all the thoughts out of your head.

"What would you girls like to do?" my mother asked. Nobody had any ideas.

"Would you like to go for a walk?" she tried next, but they looked at each other and shook their heads.

"Let's play hide and seek," Susan suggested. Diana agreed with her at once. I felt uneasy. There is something sly about Susan. I've never really trusted her. I could imagine the whispering in the bushes and the giggling in dark corners.

But my mother was taken in by her doll's face, with its round red cheeks and wide-open blue eyes. She thought Susan was a nice child and hide-and-seek an innocent, old-fashioned game.

"What a good idea," she said. "You can use both the house and the garden to hide in. Only not the study or the kitchen, please." She then volunteered to be the first "it."

Everyone hid in the garden at first. I was able to keep near Rosie, crouching behind the same bush or behind a neighboring tree. I don't know why I felt it necessary to protect her. She was two years older than any of us and used to holding her own in a tough world. But somehow I was worried.

When my mother went in to see about tea, Susan

said it was my turn to be "it." She and Diana were smiling. I didn't like the look on their faces.

"Let's play something else," I said. "I'm bored with hide-and-seek."

They wouldn't let me get away with that. It wasn't fair, they said. Everyone else had been "it." Now it was my turn. "And mind you count to a hundred and don't peek."

I cheated. Looking through my fingers, I saw Rosie go into the house. I saw Susan and Diana tiptoe after her. I waited until Charlotte had hidden herself behind the rhododendrons and then, although I had only counted to thirty, I ran into the house.

They would be upstairs, I thought, as far away from my mother as possible. I looked first in my room, worried about my wardrobe and the hidden parcel, but they were undisturbed. I looked in Rosie's room. No one there.

Then I heard voices along the passage. Someone was shouting. As I walked towards the sound, the door of the spare room suddenly opened and Rosie came out. She gave me a brief glance and then turned to look back into the room. Over her shoulder I saw Susan and Diana standing close together, looking like children who have succeeded in provoking a caged animal and were now worried in case the bars wouldn't hold.

"We were only—" Susan began, but Rosie swore at her.

"You stupid beggars, you want your heads examined. You don't know nothing. Mum's not like that. Did she beat me? Did she starve me? Gawd, what rubbish! This ain't a fairy story—what d'you take my mum for? The wicked witch? Did she keep me chained in a cellar? How daft can you get! I'll tell you something, Mum gave me more freedom than you soft lot will ever know. And as for this poor kid here"—she jerked her thumb at me—"it's a wonder she's allowed to blow her own nose."

With that, she brushed past me and ran downstairs. I watched her out of sight and then turned back to Susan and Diana.

"We weren't being horrid, honestly, Kate," Susan said.

"We didn't ask her anything. We didn't!" Diana agreed. "We just wanted to sympathize. What's wrong with that?"

"I only said it must have been horrid for her being kidnapped like that."

"We thought she'd think it odd if we didn't show *any* interest."

"We were only trying to be nice, that's all."

"She swore at us," Susan said. "She used that word, you know."

"And we weren't even nasty back."

There seemed no point in quarreling with them.

"It can't be helped," I said. "Only . . . she was fond of her mum, you see."

They came closer to me, relieved I wasn't cross with them.

"Is she really your sister, Kate?"

"She doesn't look a bit like you."

"Perhaps she's a changeling. Perhaps that woman's trying to plant her own daughter on you. I mean, she's a bit weird, isn't she?"

"That awful blouse," Susan said, and giggled.

"And that hair!"

"She doesn't seem our sort at all. You don't like her, do you, Kate?"

I should have stopped them at once. I should have said very loudly, "Yes, I do like her. I like her very much. Better than I like you two cats." But I didn't. I don't know why not. Except that they were my friends and no worse, after all, than I had been.

I hesitated too long. Susan's eyes widened suddenly, looking over my shoulder in alarm.

I turned round. Rosie was behind me. I saw at once from her face that she had heard too much. Too much and not enough.

"Your mum sent me to say tea's ready," she said, and walked away.

I tried to explain later when they had gone. I tried to apologize.

"It's all right," she said, her face expressionless. "It doesn't matter now. Don't worry. Leave it alone."

That night she ran away.

21

A hideous metallic screaming woke me out of my sleep. I sat up in bed, my heart thumping. The sound went on and on, shrill and harsh. I could not think what it was, yet somehow it seemed familiar, as if I had heard it before. Perhaps in a nightmare.

Footsteps hurrying . . . my mother's voice, high-pitched and nervous, "Don't! No, don't . . ."

I ran out onto the landing. My mother and father were looking over the banisters. The lights were on. Down below, the hall was bright and empty. The front door was ajar and the burglar alarm ringing.

"Stay here," my father said. "I'll just check—"

"No, don't go down, Anthony. Ring the police from our room. Please." My mother was holding his arm. Her fear infected me. I was terrified of burglars. I clung to him, crying. They'd have guns. They'd shoot him.

He tried to loosen my fingers from his arm, telling me not to be silly. "They won't be here now, not with that damned row going on. The whole street must be awake—"

Except Rosie?

Her door was behind me. I opened it and switched on the light. The room was empty, the bed made. It looked as if no one had ever slept there. In the wardrobe, the dresses my mother had given her still hung untouched on their hangers—Emma's dresses, not Rosie's. Only the things she had brought with her had gone.

My mother was crying.

I ran down the stairs and out of the house. The gravel pricked my bare feet, and my nightdress flapped round me like a sail in the wind. Outside on the pavement I looked up and down the road. There was no sign of Rosie.

Then I felt my father's arm round my shoulder. He was in his pajamas, gray and white stripes in the moonlight. My mother was shivering behind him.

"I'll take the car," he said. "She can't have gone far."

Light came on in an upstairs window in the house next door. A curtain moved, spilling out a brighter oblong of gold. A silhouetted head appeared and looked down at us. Our neighbor, Mr. Barrington. He opened the window wider and called out, "Is everything all right?"

What did he think we were doing in the windy moonlight, dressed only in our nightclothes?

I left my father to explain. "Get dressed," he'd said as he pushed me towards the house.

I rushed up to my room. When I came down again, in trousers and parka, my parents were in the hall. My father had put an old raincoat over his pajamas and shoes on his bare feet.

"Good," he said when he saw me.

"You're not taking Kate with you, Anthony?"

"Yes. Her eyes are sharper than mine. The Barringtons are coming over in a minute—you'll be all right till then, won't you?"

"I want to come," my mother said, but my father said someone had to stay in case Rosie came back. Someone she knew.

"Give me half an hour," he said. "If we haven't found her by then, we'll have to get on to the police."

We drove towards the corner. The moon was round and bright, and cast deep shadows. Our headlights lit them briefly, and passed on. Once I thought I saw a pair of pale legs gleaming in a dark doorway, but it was only two empty milk bottles, side by side.

"Surely she must have known we had a burglar alarm," my father said.

"I didn't tell her. Did you?"

"No. You'd think she'd have noticed."

"I shouldn't think she's used to them. What's that?"

"Where?"

Two eyes glared, green as emeralds—a black cat out hunting.

We turned into Heath Street. There was a man on the pavement, dark coat, dark hair, silver face made sinister by the night. Another figure, head bent, hurried along with his hands in his pockets. I shivered. The empty streets had been less frightening than this one of slinking shadows. I thought of Rosie, alone in the dark, running and running, with nowhere to go to. . . .

"Nowhere"—she had said that. She'd run away

once before, she'd told me—"Then I thought, where the hell am I going? Nowhere. So I hid . . ."

"Daddy," I cried. "I know where she'll be!"

Rosie was standing outside Hampstead Underground Station, peering through the locked metal gates. Her three carrier-bags were on the pavement by her feet. Although she must have heard the car stopping, she did not turn round, but flattened herself against the grille as if hoping to disappear.

Then I was out of the car with my arms round her. "Rosie!"

She tried to free herself, but I held on tightly till my father came.

"Rosie, come home," he said gently. "Please come home."

"Leave me alone," she muttered, and kicked the metal gates furiously, making them rattle and shake. "Why the hell are they locked?"

"It's nearly two o'clock. There are no trains running now. Please come home, my dear."

Her voice rose hysterically. "You can't make me! 'Oo d'you think you are. Go away, will you!"

She picked up her carrier-bags and started walking on. My father caught her up and took hold of her arm. She kicked his ankle, struggling and swearing.

We were on the corner now. I could see down Haverstock Hill. In the distance a blue light was flashing.

"Daddy, look!"

They both saw the flashing light.

"The police," Rosie said. She sounded half frightened, half gleeful. "If you don't let me go, I'll tell them you're kidnapping me. I will! Molesting me, that's what I'll say, molesting. You'll be in trouble. I hope they put you in jail. You got no rights. You ain't my dad."

"He is! He is!" I babbled. Behind them I could see the blue light approaching. "I've got proof . . . a parcel, a parcel from your mum."

They were both staring at me now.

"I'll tell you in the car," I said. "Hurry up!"

We were only just in time. As my father drew away from the curb, we saw the police car sweep past us and vanish up the hill. My father drove on.

"You ain't taking me back," Rosie said. "I'll jump out first."

"I can park here." My father drew up, switched off the engine and the lights. Then he put on the inside light and looked at me. His face was cold and stern.

"Well, Kate. We're waiting."

"It—it came weeks ago, soon after Rosie," I said, looking away nervously, wishing I had more time to think. "A parcel . . . I was in the front and the postman gave it to me. It was for Rosie—at least, it said Miss Emma Seton, but I recognized the writing from that letter and . . . and I opened it."

"*What?*"

"I'm sorry. I'm sorry. I didn't mean to, but . . . I was jealous, I suppose. I didn't want Rosie to stay, not then." I was crying now, real tears ran down my cheeks. I no longer felt as if I were acting. "It's at home. I'll show it to you. The parcel . . . I can't show you the letter. I—I tore it up. I tore it up and flushed it down the loo. But I've still got the parcel. I've still got the proof. It's hidden in my wardrobe."

I could see from their faces that they believed me. They thought it was just the sort of thing I would do. It was in character. I was hurt by this, and yet, in an odd way, it *was* true, even though it hadn't happened. I had been that sort of person once. I had torn up a photograph.

"This proof, what is it?" my father asked.

"I'll show you," I said. "When we get home." Then I began to cry loudly so that they couldn't question me anymore.

I'd forgotten the Barringtons would be there. There were too many people in the hall, welcoming us, hugging and kissing and exclaiming. Hot soup ready in the kitchen, hot milk on offer . . .

Rosie let it all wash round her. She did not say a word. Her dark eyes were fixed on me.

The Barringtons did not stay long. As soon as they had gone, I said, "I'll get the parcel. Stay here. I'll bring it down."

It was no good. They followed me upstairs. I could hear my mother asking, "What parcel? What is she talking about?"

I did not want them to come. The parcel was wrapped up and tied with string. But there was no stamp. No postmark.

"Sit on the bed," I said. "Over there. I'll get it."

They wouldn't sit down. They stood and watched me as I took my chair and put it in front of the wardrobe.

"Is it up there? Let me get it," my father said.

"No. I can do it."

I was standing on the chair now, opening the top of my wardrobe, reaching inside my sleeping bag on the high shelf. My fingers felt paper and string. I tried to tear them off.

"Kate, what are you doing?" my father said sharply. He stepped forward and lifted me down from the chair. The parcel fell to the floor.

Rosie reached it first. The string was dangling now and the paper half torn off. Kneeling on the floor, she ripped it open. And there it was, the teddy bear. Dirty, smudged with dust and stained with cold tea, a frayed pink ribbon round its neck, it stared up with its innocent, embroidered eyes.

Silence. Not a flicker of recognition on any face.

Then Rosie said, "What the flipping hell is that supposed to be?"

I could have hit her. "It's the teddy bear! The teddy bear!" I turned to my mother. "The one Emma had. You know, the one in the photograph."

"Photograph?"

"Yes!" I shouted angrily. Why were they all so stupid? I ran to my dressing table and took the photograph out of my trinket box. "Here, this one—look!" I held it out. "There it is, see? Emma's teddy bear."

"But, darling, that's not Emma," my mother said, looking bewildered. "That's your little cousin Jane, when she stayed—"

My father had been watching me, an odd expression in his eyes. He stepped forward suddenly and took the photograph out of my mother's hand.

"Don't be silly, Margaret," he said. "Of course it's Emma. I ought to know. I took it myself. Yes, and I remember the teddy bear. Elizabeth gave it to her. You remember now, Margaret, don't you?"

Their eyes met. Then my mother said quickly, "Yes. How silly of me. Of course I remember. The toy must have been in her pram when—"

" 'Oo d'you think you're kidding?" Rosie asked. She had been watching our charade, her eyes going from one face to another; too sharp, too knowing. "It ain't even old. Look at it!" She picked up the bear and pulled it this way and that. Patches of white showed too brightly through the artificial stains. She flicked the pink ribbon with her finger. "It ain't even faded. You

silly kid, you made it yourself," she said, looking at me.
"Not much good at knitting, are you?"

I felt like crying. Everything had gone wrong, and I
had tried so hard.

"Rosie—" my mother began, but my father put his
hand on her arm, and she was silent.

Rosie was still looking at me. There was an odd
expression in her face. She held the bear in her hands,
turning it over and over in thin, nervous fingers, but
her eyes never left me.

She said slowly, "So that's why you locked yourself
in your room . . . that's what you were up to all those
days . . ." She made it sound a long, weary time.
"*Why?* What did you do it for, Kate?"

"For you," I mumbled. "I wanted you to stay. I
don't care who you are. I want you to stay."

"You mean—'ooever I am?"

"Yes."

She put the bear suddenly up to her face. I don't
know if she heard my father say that we all wanted her,
that we loved her for herself. I think she was crying. My
mother knelt down beside her and put her arms round
her, and for the first time, Rosie did not pull away.

"Will you stay?" I asked.

She sniffed and did not answer. Then she rubbed
the toy over her face like a dirty handkerchief, leaving
dusty smudges on her wet cheeks.

"Suppose I might as well be your Emma," she said.
"After all, what's in a name?"

22

I wanted to end it like that. It still seems to me the right ending. That was the night we became a family; the four of us sitting round the table, drinking hot soup at three o'clock in the morning. That was the night we first started calling her Emma (at least when we remembered to). That was the night my father was proud of me, and when Rosie first called him "Dad"—a little doubtfully, as if she was trying a hat on him that might not fit. (It took her much longer to call my mother anything. She calls her Ma now. I suppose Mum for her will always be that shadowy woman with red or yellow hair.) That night, the empty chair on the fourth side of the table no longer haunted us. Emma had come home.

She is still here, my older sister. Emma is seventeen now and I am fifteen. Four years have passed, four years in which we have grown up. Noisily. Tempestuously. Our house is no longer quiet and dull and respectable behind its high walls. Battles rage like thunder through the rooms and, like thunder, clear the air.

My mother says that having two daughters does not halve her worries but doubles them; and my father, once so cold and calm and reasonable, shouts at us. Then he feels ashamed of himself and apologizes. But they are happier now. At times they are almost lively, like tortoises emerging after a long winter. As for Emma and me, we laugh and quarrel all over the house. At the tops of our voices.

Mrs. Trapp, who is still with us, complains of the noise we make. But she comforts my mother that the worst is over. "They'll be working hard for their exams, that'll keep them quiet," she says. "After all, it was bound to take them time to settle down. I mean, being brought up so different. You can see they're really very fond of each other, can't you, Mrs. Seton? I dunno when I've seen sisters so close, in spite of all the shouting that goes on."

Today they will be pleased with us. We are not making a noise. We are sitting side by side on the window seat in the playroom, and Emma is reading my manuscript while I watch her nervously and bite my fingernails.

"You can't end it like that," she says.

"Why not?"

"It's unfinished. You haven't said who I turned out to be."

"That's the whole point," I explain patiently. "It doesn't matter. You are you. You don't need a label. There are too many labels in this world."

"Tell that to the postman. The Cuckoo Sister, indeed!"

I suppose I look bitterly disappointed, for she smiles and says, "You finish it properly. Give them the facts, and then I'll praise it. Perhaps."

This is how we found out who she was. Six weeks after the night of the teddy bear, someone came knocking at our door like a bolt from the blue. Except that bolt suggests something hard and he was soft and fleshy, a huge shambling man, with a round red face framed in curly hair, like the sun in a wig.

Emma and I did not see him arrive. We had been out for a walk. When we came back, he was already there, sitting on a chair that now seemed too small, and having tea with my parents. The delicate cup looked uneasy in his huge hands.

He got to his feet when we came in, spilling some of the tea into the saucer.

" 'Ullo, Rosie, love," he said nervously. " 'Ow've you been keeping?"

"*You!*"

"Yeh, it's me—"

"What d'you want?"

"Me and your—and Louise are married now," he blurted out, with a mixture of pride and apprehension, looking as if he expected Emma to throw something at him. I think my father thought so too, for he put his hand on her shoulder warningly, and said, "Mr. Jenkins has very kindly come to—to put the record straight."

I was not surprised to hear his name. I had recognized him right away. The man at the gate. Harry Jenkins. The hairy ape who had broken the bingo vase. I don't suppose he meant to. He looked kind. I couldn't think why Rosie hated him so.

"Felt I 'ad to come. Only right," he was saying gratefully, when Emma interrupted him.

"Where's Mum?"

Mr. Jenkins looked apologetically at her. "That's what I come to say, Rosie, love. Miss Emma, I suppose I should say. She ain't your mum. Mrs. Seton's your mother, and that's the truth. It's all there." He gestured toward the table. Beside the plate of biscuits there were some documents.

"Where's Mum?" Rosie said again, and then added bitterly, "Where's Mrs. Harry Jenkins?"

"Not very well, Rosie, I'm sorry to say. Got one of 'er 'eadaches."

"Yeh. That's her all over. Gets into trouble and then hides under the bed."

"Now, you don't want to say that. She's 'ad a bad time, 'as Louise. Done nothing but cry for weeks—ever since the wedding," he added a little ruefully. "Well, I could tell there was something wrong, couldn't I? That's when I got it out of her. What she done, I mean. Took me back, I can tell you. 'Owever she come to do it . . . well, it beats me. But there's excuses. Like your dad says, we mustn't be too 'ard on 'er. She's ever so sorry for what she done. She asked me to give you 'er love—"

"Love!"

"She misses you," he said simply.

Rosie turned away. My mother took her hand and pulled her gently down onto the sofa. My father took Mr. Jenkins's cup, tipped out the tea that had spilled on to the saucer, and refilled it for him. We all sat down. I chose the chair nearest the table on which the papers were. Out of the corner of my eye I saw they were certificates of some sort. Under the pretense of choosing a biscuit I edged them nearer.

"That's right, love, you look at them," Mr. Jenkins said, putting down his cup and coming over to me. "And you too, Rosie, love. It's all 'ere." He picked up the papers and held one out to us. "This one's 'er birth certificate, see? Louise Edwards she was born and Louise Edwards she was when she married me. She called 'erself Louise Martin for a bit, but it was never 'er real name. Though your dad says it's legal, mind."

"Yes," my father said. "It is not compulsory to change your name by deed poll."

Mr. Jenkins was holding out another certificate. "This is 'er poor baby's," he said.

It was a birth certificate for Rose Edwards, daughter of Louise Edwards, born on July thirty-first. Father unknown.

Emma looked up sharply, and Mr. Jenkins said hastily, "No, no! I 'adn't even met your mum then. Louise, I mean. I wish I 'ad. I'd 'ave seen 'er through 'er trouble. Comforted 'er when the poor little beggar died. She'd never 'ave done what she did if I'd been there."

I liked him very much then. He was holding the next paper in his hand, hesitating, as if he thought a death certificate too sad a thing to show young girls like us. "She was only five weeks old," he said.

"She died?" Emma asked. "You mean, Rosie died?"

He nodded. "On September fourth. She 'ad something wrong with 'er. The doctors couldn't save her."

Rosie was silent. Her face was very pale. I wondered what it was like, finding out you were someone else. Finding out that the child you had thought you were had died when it was only five weeks old. She had been one woman's dream—and another woman's nightmare. No wonder she looked like a ghost.

"You're Emma. You're my sister," I whispered. "I always knew you were."

"I should of let you know right away," Mr. Jenkins said, wiping his brow with a large handkerchief. "I wanted to, but Louise was frightened. . . . I did come once, but only as far as the gate." He turned to me. "You must of thought it queer, miss. Me rushing off like that."

They were all staring at me.

"Lost my nerve," he explained sheepishly. "I 'adn't expected a 'ouse like this. Louise should of warned me."

"I don't understand," my father said. "Have you and Kate met before?"

"Yeh. Well, not to say met. I just asked if Rosie lived 'ere—"

"You didn't!" I protested quickly. "You said it

wasn't Rosie. You said it was some other little girl you wanted. You know you did."

"Well, like I said, I got cold feet," he said, looking embarrassed.

"Why didn't you tell us, Kate?" my father asked.

I didn't know. I couldn't remember. I knew I had had some reason that had seemed good at the time, but I had forgotten it.

"He said it wasn't Rosie he was looking for," I mumbled.

"My fault," Mr. Jenkins said generously. He thanked my mother for the tea. Then he turned to my father and shook him heartily by the hand. "I can't thank you enough, sir, for being so understanding. It'll set poor Louise's mind at rest. She was frightened you'd 'ave her put in prison. You won't regret it, I promise you. I'll take good care she don't do nothing silly again. We're hoping to 'ave kids of our own soon." Rosie drew in her breath sharply, and he turned to look at her with awkward kindness. "They won't never take your place, love, but you're better with your own folks. I'll say good-bye, then." He held out his hand a little nervously, as if afraid she'd bite it. I thought at first she was going to refuse to take it, but in the end she shook it briefly and then wiped her hand on her skirt.

"Good-bye, then," he said again. My father walked with him to the door. Mr. Jenkins hesitated, half in and half out of the room. "I don't know 'ow to say it. I suppose it seems cheek, like," he said.

We waited, puzzled.

"I mean, I'll understand if you won't 'ear of it. But I promised I'd ask."

"Yes?"

"It's just—Louise wondered if she could see Rosie before we go off. Just to say good-bye. You see, we're off to Australia next month. Emigrating. So, well, it'd be just to say good-bye. I dunno 'ow you feel about it?"

I could have told him. They were glad he was emigrating. Sorry it wasn't sooner. Tomorrow. Or better still, this afternoon.

"I think it must be Emma's decision," my father said slowly.

It seemed a long silence while we waited for her to answer. Then she mumbled, "Yeh. I'd like to see her." She glanced at my mother and added, "If that's all right with you, Ma?"

"Yes, of course, darling. I understand." She turned to Mr. Jenkins. "When would she like to come?"

"I dunno that she'd feel able to come 'ere," Mr. Jenkins said, looking horribly embarrassed. "I don't think she could bring 'erself to face you, ma'am. She's that ashamed—and so she should be. I was thinking we could meet in some caff. 'Ere in 'Ampstead, if you'd agree. I'd see 'er safe back."

My mother looked worried. I could see my father did not like it either. He was frowning.

"I'll come back, Dad," Emma said quickly. "I'll come back home."

She was very quiet when Mr. Jenkins brought her back. That night I heard her crying in her room. I sat up in bed, wondering if I should go and comfort her, but not certain if she would want me. She was crying for her mum. For Louise. I knew that. I did not think she would want any of us now.

I sat listening to her cry. It was a small, lonely sound in the night. Many times I got out of bed, meaning to go to her, but then hesitated. At last I could hear her no more. I tiptoed into her room. She had cried herself to sleep. The cloudy moonlight was shifting over her face, changing it endlessly from silver to shadow.

Looking down at her, I knew there would always be a part of her I could not share. A stranger. Somewhere inside her, the cuckoo sister would live on. I would see Rosie looking out at me from Emma's eyes. Just as in me, there'd always be the ghost of a spoilt child who had been so jealous. I suppose we all have hidden selves. You can't get away from secrets, can you?

I watched her for a long time. I felt happy. Her cheeks were still wet with Rosie's tears, but my sister was holding tightly in her arms the teddy bear I had knitted for her, like a talisman for the future.